Published by Stuart Kenyon 2019

For Vicky, Max and Poppy

Chapter 1 — Luke Norman — 9:45

It's a hacking, wet, coughing sound, as if someone's choking on their own blood. Are they in their death throes, stricken by a terrible disease? Mortally wounded, spluttering their last breaths?

No, it's just Mary, who wouldn't take a day off if she won the lottery, battling through the pain to serve the company's ungrateful consumers.

Luke shakes his head. *If yer gonna die,* he thinks, *do it quietly. Some of us 'ave 'eadaches.*

His earpiece beeps.

"Good morning," he begins, "you're through to Luke at Union Energy, how can I —"

"— 'Duke'?" the elderly caller splutters. "I'm through t' *Duke*?"

"No, sorry sir." Luke isn't sorry. It's not his fault the old guy's deaf. "My name is Luke, at Union Energy. How can I help?"

"I keep gettin' bloody missed calls from you lot, 'n' I don't know why. *You're* not my supplier. Norweb are. Now pack it in!"

"Okay. If I can just take some details —"

"— No, ya can't. Just stop ringin' me!"

The line goes dead.

Sighing, Luke presses the 'not ready' button on his phone to prevent another call coming through. It's much busier than usual, even for a Monday. Less than an hour into his shift, he's already taken six inbounds. Five of them have been pensioners; most people use web chat these days.

Too many employees have rung in sick today. It's hot outside, only late May but close to 30°C. No doubt many of his peers are in the beer gardens of Mortborough or nearby Manchester. *Lucky bastards.* A storm is forecast for later, however. Naturally, the rain is meant to start just as Luke's shift finishes. Judging by the clouds on the horizon, the heavens will open sooner, much sooner.

Knuckling his eyes, he contemplates taking the next call. Sometimes the dread of speaking to another irate customer is a palpable thing. He's hungover today, feeling as bad as he looks, so the terror's worse. Another weekend wasted, another wage frittered. *You're pathetic*, his ex's voice rattles in his head. *Yeah, I might be pathetic, but if you'd just let me see Connor, I'd get my act together —*

"Tough morning?" Geraint, sitting next to Luke, chirps. He favours a bushy moustache in defiance of fashion; its ginger strands have snared a crumb of breakfast.

"Too busy." Luke smiles tightly. He always tries to be nice to Geraint, but something about the forty year-old is troubling.

"Did you see your kid this weekend? Your boy?" Geraint looks at the digital photo frame featuring the child in question.

"Not this week. I'm gonna grab a brew. Want one?"

"No, thank you."

Walking away from his workstation, Luke laments his decision not to don shorts this morning. The call centre is humid and smells musty. It's too brightly lit, full of people who would rather be anywhere else. Row upon row of desks, a sweaty prison of plastic and cheap carpets. The kitchen is a sanctuary for tormented souls, but respite is always short-lived. Twenty minutes a day is the allowance for personal breaks, and Luke has already used 203 seconds.

While waiting for his tea to brew, Luke worries at an ingrown hair on his stubbled jaw. Suddenly he remembers: his new inhaler. He pulls the cigar-shaped device from his pocket and takes a hit. Glancing around self-consciously, he sees Brad at the water cooler. "Hey, Brad."

"Alright, bro." His friend is thirty-one, the same age as Luke. "Fuckin' busy today, innit?"

"Awful. Why are these sad bastard customers ringin' us when they could be outside in the sun?"

"Fuck knows." Brad sips his H^2O and places it on one of the chest high break tables. "Screw it." He perches on a stool. "I'm takin' five. Don't care if the bosses kick off."

Luke chuckles and takes a seat next to his colleague. "You not warm, mate?" He nods at the other man's hoodie.

"Tropical blood, bro. In Singapore, 30 C ain't nothin'." Brad pulls an inhaler, identical to Luke's, from his own pocket, and takes a toke.

"Yeah, I guess. Not even that hot fer Manchester these days, is it? I think the Earth's gettin' us back fer starting the Industrial Revolution." He holds his inhaler aloft. "How long you been on this shit now?"

"Week or so. You?"

"Same, I think… yeah, it was last Monday I went to the doctor's, but I got the call the Friday before. Fucked up though, innit? GP's don't usually call *you* in to give ya new meds, do they?"

"No. Same with me, Friday call, docs on Monday."

"Ya reckon they've done the same to everyone with allergies? Geraint on my team's got 'ayfever, like me, 'n' he's 'ad 'is changed. Tia's in, 'n' I'm pretty sure she's got asthma, like you."

"Dunno. Probably some scam wi' the big pharma companies. They're corrupt as fuck. I was readin' this article on 'Counter-Clockwise' the other day —"

"— Shit, Brad," Luke cuts in, "you're not on the dark web again, are ya? Ya know what'll happen if ya get caught doin' that at work?"

"Nah, I cover my tracks well. Perks of bein' an IT genius, 'n' all." The smaller Asian man cranes his neck to look over his friend's shoulder. "Jesus. Alicia's dropped from a nine outta ten to a five. Look."

Luke turns: the blonde, usually immaculate, is pale, red-eyed, holding a tissue to her nose and half-trotting towards the bathrooms. "What the fuck's goin' on?" he asks as someone else nearby sneezes twice in quick succession. "It's like the bubonic plague or somethin'. People droppin' like flies, left, right 'n' centre."

"I don't know, mate, but I'm not complainin'. Most of the managers are ill, so we can chill fer as long as we want."

"Don't think so." Luke sips his tea and wonders why he's drinking hot beverages during a heatwave. "They'll be back. Then they'll check our call stats, 'n' we'll be up shit creek. I'd best get back."

Brad shrugs and takes his phone from his pocket. "See you at lunch?"

"Yep. I'm skipping food today, though. I'm skint till payday."

"Me too, bro. It's eight quid for a shitty sandwich from the canteen now."

"Jesus! It only went up t' seven last month. Catch ya later, anyway."

Luke heads back to his area, which is somehow even less populated now than it was ten minutes earlier. Dependable – *yet weird* – Geraint is still holding the fort, of course, but Marco and Amerie's places are newly-vacant. An unease settles in Luke's gut, and it isn't the previous day's beer. *Should he be at work, wi' so many falling ill? What if he catches the disease 'n' infects Connor?*

Luke snorts to himself. He would have to actually see his son to pass anything on to him. It's three weeks and counting since the last time he hugged his eleven year-old boy, thanks to the kid's mother. Sitting in his faulty chair, Luke exhales at length. He clicks the 'ready' button and braces himself for the next idiot.

Nobody.

"It's gone quiet," Geraint says. "Think it might be a fault with the phone lines. I'm on hold to IT now to check, but no one's answering."

"Not surprised. They're probably all sick too." *Or takin' liberties, like Brad.*

"It's really weird, innit, Luke?" Tia, a plump teenaged brunette, calls from a neighbouring team. "Plus, the people who're off sick, most of 'em 'aven't rung in, like. That's what *I* 'eard."

Luke frowns; Tia's gossip isn't the best of sources. "What, you mean they're 'AWOL'?"

"Yeah. Disciplinary shit, innit, but they can't sack *everyone*, can they, like?"

"Suppose not." Luke looks around the office. He's never seen it so empty. The atmosphere is strange, too; there's a paranoia, or is that simply the remnants of last night's cheap vodka taunting him? He almost wishes for the beep in his headset, even if it's another grouchy old man: anything to stop his mind playing tricks. Wiping a sheen of sweat from his brow, he wakes his monitor by moving the computer's mouse and tries surfing the web to distract himself. The football news is a blur on the screen, though. The bright colours of an online game don't hold his attention, either.

Tia's just been talking to one of her teammates, but now she's looking at Luke again. "'Ave *you* noticed that?"

"What?"

She brandishes her own inhaler as if it's the holy grail. "Everyone who's in today is on one o' these."

"She isn't," Geraint says quietly, tipping his head back towards the elevators.

It's obvious to whom he's referring: Mary. Although the middle-aged woman is seated at least thirty feet away, her discomfort is plain. Her complexion is grey, the shaking of her hands visible.

"Yeah," Tia argues, "'n' look at the state of 'er! She's literally dyin'. I'm going nowhere near 'er, I'm tellin' ya. Look, she's sweatin' buckets!"

"Shh!" Luke hisses. "She can't 'elp being ill, can she?"

"No, but she should be at 'ome, not spreadin' germs all over the place."

The aforementioned pillar of the call centre is coughing again, and even from this distance, the wheezes that follow every fit are audible.

Somebody should take a look at her. "Is there no one first aid trained about?" Luke stands. Licks his lips. "Someone should, ya know, see if she needs any 'elp."

Everyone looks elsewhere.

Fer fucksake. Squeezing the nape of his neck, Luke approaches the ailing woman. He wrinkles his nose at the sharp tang of perspiration. At the moment, she's the only person in the complaints department, which has a canal-side view. It's quiet outside, especially considering the sunshine. "Ah, Mary?"

She looks at him as if he's the Grim Reaper. Up close, her condition is even more concerning. Blood flecks her chin; her conservative beige blouse is damp with drool.

"It's okay, Mary. Do you want a glass of water, maybe?

No reply.

"Should I call someone for ya? Family, friend, or somethin'? Doctor?"

Her head shakes, but is she answering 'no' or having a seizure?

Suddenly, she erupts into another round of racking gasps and wheezes. But on this occasion, she doesn't stop coughing after twenty seconds. Her ordeal continues until she gives one final heave and spews a slug-sized wad of crimson mucous onto her computer keyboard. A fine, bloody spray showers Luke's hand, which he was just about to place on her shoulder. A couple of droplets land on his white polo-shirt, too.

He recoils. "Help! Someone, help!"

Mary's turning blue. Then purple.

Horrified, her would-be aide stares as others gather around. "I didn't touch 'er! She just… she just…"

"Fuckin' 'ell.' Tia's covering her mouth with one orange-tanned hand. "I saw it, Luke."

"Does anyone know CPR?" he asks the floor in general.

He might as well be speaking Mongolian, for no one replies. Nine people, including Brad, who's comes to bear witness, are fixated on Mary and Luke. The tenth, an ex-plumber by the name of Cal, is on the phone. He's describing Mary's symptoms, so he's presumably summoning paramedics.

"Is there nobody else 'ere?" Luke begs. "Brad, go t' the second floor, see if someone up there —"

The door to the mezzanine flies open. One of the second floor managers, a stick-thin fellow named Barry, stumbles into view. "Is anyone here first aid-trained? Anyone?"

The dazed inhabitants of Union Energy's customer service department blink at the newcomer.

"Wait!" Barry hurries over. "You lot have one too?"

Still transfixed by Mary's suffering, Luke nods. "Someone on third, maybe?" He feels detached all of a sudden. As though he's watching events unfold on TV.

"Tried them. They've got two like her. I'll try first." Barry spins on his heel and heads for the staircase.

"Cal," Brad calls. "Any joy?"

The burly fellow has just hung up. "They said we're looking at an hour's wait, at least."

"An *hour*?" several chorus.

"Yeah. They're mad-busy, they reckon. Loadsa fuckers like 'er, probably."

So Mary dies. In the end, she goes relatively peacefully, but that doesn't stop the other women present – and one of the men – breaking into sobs.

"Shit." Luke says after finding no pulse. "I need some fresh air."

Brad follows him down the stairway. They cross the deathly-silent lobby, which hasn't been cleaned today. There's no security guard on duty, either. Outside and into the patchy sunshine they go; they sit on a mouldy bench in the smoking enclosure. For a few heartbeats Luke enjoys the rays on his face. Then he remembers Mary's dead face, and his head drops.

"I know." Brad's rolling a cigarette. He's filling it with cannabis, not tobacco. "It's fucked up. But there's nothin' we could do."

Luke stares at imitation flowers in a plant pot, watching the plastic stems shift in a wind that's getting stronger. Somewhere, not too far away, something is burning. He vapes nicotine, then accepts a hit on Brad's joint. "Could we catch it? Whatever Mary's got."

"Dunno, bro."

"But I could pass it onto Connor."

"Yeah. I got a kid too, remember."

Luke puffs his cheeks. "Guess we better go back upstairs. Wait fer the ambulance."

The lift's jammed again. As the two workmates climb the stairs, a scream sounds.

"Fuck." Luke gulps. He wipes grit from his eyes. "Our floor?"

"Yeah. Or third." Quickening his pace, Brad overtakes his buddy.

Another yell, this time the bass of a male. A commotion.

Brad barges his way through the heavy fire door and stops dead. "Oh, god. Oh fuck."

"What?" Luke pants. "What now?" He skirts the smaller man's stationary frame and stares.

Mary died. The coughing stopped; she stopped breathing; her heart stopped pumping.

So why is she on 'er feet? Why is she twitchin' like a shit dancer? Why is she lungin' for Cal 'n' grabbin' 'im by the shoulders? Why is she bitin' 'is face?

It doesn't make sense. But that doesn't stop her turning away from her screeching victim – with slick, dark gore coating her mouth, chin and M & S shirt – and lurching towards her former co-workers.

Chapter 2 — Jada Blakowska — 10:20

"For godsake!"

"Pardon?" Gracie exclaims via the hatchback's hands-free phone speaker.

"Sorry, hun," Jada says. "Just some idiot in a self-driven car, cutting me up. You were saying?"

"I'm sorry about the other day, that's all. I shouldn't have lost my temper."

"Oh, don't worry! I'm used to you and your —" Jada slams on the brakes as the van in front does likewise "—*ways*. God, the roads are horrendous today."

"Bad weather's coming, I hear. It's already thundering here in the city centre, what about there?"

"Not yet. But I'm still fifteen miles away."

"What do you mean, anyway, you cheeky monkey? I don't have 'ways.'"

"Yes, you do."

Gracie adopts a mock-haughty tone: "You're talking your way out of me buying brunch, Jada dearest."

"Don't be daft, you! It's my turn to buy today." Jada stops at another temporary traffic light. "So, have you thought about the article…"

"*Hmm*. We'll talk about it properly when we eat. You're meeting me at eleven, right? Traffic's horrific, by the way. Another one of those bloody climate change rallies, as if they can make a difference these days. One of their targets is Evolve, funnily enough."

"Shame we didn't listen to them years ago."

"I know, I know. Jacobia, Deansgate?"

"Yeah, if it's still open by the time I get there! It's bumper-to-bumper on the A9015." The twenty-seven year-old freelance journalist takes advantage of the delay and checks her hair in the mirror. Her roots need touching up; there's too much of the African jet black inherited from her mother rebelling against the blonde dye. But at least her eyebrows are freshly-threaded. Her powder blue jeans and cream shoestring-strap top are brand new, as are her on-trend sandals. "I just think it'll make a really good story, that's all."

Gracie clears her throat. "You said that the other day."

"When you shouted at me?"

"Yes, which I shouldn't have done. But I stand by my point…"

"Why, though? Evolve are dirty. You know that. I know that. They have too many ties with the last company to get the regen contract. One of the directors *owned* the last company, for godsake. Plus they're too cosy with the Government —"

"— Which is precisely why you shouldn't get involved again, Jada. You could make some powerful enemies."

The younger woman applies the brakes once more. She expects more traffic cones, but the delay isn't roadwork related: it looks like an accident. "So be it. If politicians are allowin' private companies to break laws just for personal gain, they're the sort of enemies I *want*. Anyway, are you saying you won't publish if I bring you something juicy?"

Gracie is editor-in-chief of *HotTake*, one of the UK's most successful blogsites, and she's no one's fool. 'Juicy' equals clicks. "Of course I'm not saying that." Clicks equals cash. Cash will eventually equal the house in Hale Barns she and Quentin have been eying. "I just want you to be careful, that's all."

"I know, I know. I'm always careful."

"You weren't last time, though, were you?"

"No, but I couldn't afford to be. Adderley was taking all kinds of risks with the chemicals he was proposing. Hell, he still is —"

"— Except that now, he's not the only director, is he? Evolve has a board these days."

"But they're not *above board*, are they?"

"Ha."

"Seriously, something underhanded is definitely happenin'. These plant regeneration mixtures, they might save the world, they might not. But if they're not properly tested before they're used, they could be *dangerous*. Adderley Limited failed with the last try, but no one died. It could've been worse."

"Okay, okay," Gracie chuckles. Then comes the faint sound of a door knocking, followed by a dog barking. "I surrender! We'll talk about it some more over brunch, anyway. I have to dash, there's someone with a delivery. See you at eleven."

The two friends ring off.

Jada curses. She didn't mention her best news: the dissenting source within Evolve plc whose testimony would make the scoop national headline material. News at Ten-worthy rather than Facebook-worthy.

She curses again, at length, for now she can see smoke in the distance. Perhaps the crash is a bad one. Which will mean she misses Jacobia with Gracie, though her bank balance would thank her for that – brunch cost Gracie nearly £100 the last time they went. There would be no such silver lining if she had to cancel the meeting she has arranged with Sofia Aslam, Adderley's chief scientist, however.

Also, she realises guiltily, someone might be badly hurt. Sirens are getting louder, the fumes up ahead thicker. The three lane A-road is gridlocked. Bizarrely, the opposite side of the highway is nearly as congested.

"What on earth…" Jada mutters, opening her door. The smell of her perfume is instantly masked by that of burning tyres and exhaust fumes. Emergency vehicle wails drown out the honks of impatient motorists. Before climbing out and closing the door behind herself, she grabs the new inhaler from the passenger seat and takes a hit. *Christ, that tastes like shit.*

In the east, towards the city centre, thunder rumbles. Has the storm caused the accident? If someone's died, it would be the second weather-related death in Greater Manchester since Saturday. Climate change is claiming victims in a variety of ways these days: first the bees died out; then crops started dying, meaning food shortages. Monoculture farming didn't help, either. Droughts, floods and pestilence are ravaging Britain almost as viciously as continental Europe, with the rest of the world worse. And all the while, the global population keeps growing, passing eight billion last month.

Hence the likes of Adderley winning hastily-written crop regeneration contracts.

Jada stops staring into the middle-distance and begins to pay attention to her surroundings. The Evolve splash is a lucrative one, but, as her university lecturer used to say, 'there are stories all around us, if we just open our eyes'.

Having not seen a vehicle move for at least five minutes, Jada slips between her BMW and the Audi to the rear. Now on the pavement, she heads eastwards, towards the column of black smoke. She's not on her own, either. Others are heading to investigate.

In fact, one, a strapping young male, halts and points to the west. Judging by the smoke, there's another conflagration that way. The second blaze must be bigger, and it looks like it's somewhere in Mortborough. A tingle courses the length of Jada's spine.

My home town. It has been since her Polish father and Jamaican mother married two decades ago, which is the real reason she's so focussed on exposing Evolve's villainy. Their state-of-the-art factory/laboratory is sited in the Greater Manchester suburb's industrial park. It's on her turf. Her mum and dad live a quarter mile from the sprawling granite and glass complex.

Again, Jada forces herself to focus. She continues towards Manchester, because that's where she'll find Gracie and Ms Aslam. In the distance, lightning flashes, but at least fifteen seconds pass before thunder rumbles. The sky is now steel grey, the air muggy.

Jada crests a hill, giving her a better view of the road ahead. Two hundred yards east, a fire engine is signalling to turn onto the dual carriageway. No doubt it'll use the bus lane to overtake the jammed vehicles. A police car is already in attendance, its blue lights blinking mutely. The snarl-up is caused by a collision between a small lorry and a double-decker bus, from which passengers are being conducted by the driver. Despite the volume of smoke, the fire afflicting the lorry is small. The firefighters' main job will be to extricate the lorry driver.

As Jada arrives, camera in hand, three firemen are spraying the truck's container with water. Two of their comrades apply cutting tools to the cabin, which is crumpled against the back of the bus. A high-pitched whine is accompanied by sparks and dust. The reek of burning is strong, and something else, too, something more pungent.

The journalist's eyes narrow when she notices the logo on the side of the goods vehicle: the letters of the word 'Evolve' are embossed onto five black-and-white trees.

The bus's commuters look shaken. But cuts and bruises aside, none are injured. Along with the occupants of the closest cars, they've been shepherded to a safe distance from the rapidly-diminishing fire.

Jada homes in on a short-haired middle-aged woman, who's clicking away at her cellphone, and disarms her with a sympathetic smile. "What happened?"

"I don't know. I really don't know." The lady's accent is Eastern European. "I was just watching a movie on my phone, then *bang*! That idiot rear-ends us." She points at the lorry. "I hope he's okay, though."

"Me too. Is it okay if I take your photo? I'm a reporter."

"Of course! Feel free."

Jada photographs the passenger, the damage to the bus, the fire engine and the rescue operatives. With her most flirtatious grin in place, she approaches the police officers.

"I'm sorry, Miss," a handsome, dark-skinned copper says. "You need to stay back."

"Sorry!" She stops short and lets her camera dangle at her side. "Is anyone hurt?"

"I can't really comment."

"Oh. Any idea how long we'll be stuck here for?"

"We're doin' our best."

"I'm sure *your* best will be enough." She increases her grin's wattage, then nods at the crash scene. "I hope he's okay. The driver, I mean…"

The policeman winces. "We reckon so."

"They'll probably have him out soon, right?"

"Yeah, we should 'ave things movin' again soon."

"Do you know why he crashed?"

"No. Bit of a mystery."

"Okay, thanks." Jada begins to drift away from the officer, back towards her car, but she keeps an eye on the truck. Its nearside door has been all but removed. Close by, fifty or so bus users are smoking, vaping, chatting, fiddling with their smartphones. A couple puff on inhalers like Jada's. The two cops – the Afro-Caribbean with whom Jada was speaking and a shorter, plainer white man – look bored. Their hoses now dribbling, the firefighters are leaning against their fire engine. Onlookers are losing interest and heading back to their automobiles; the first drops of rain are falling.

A loud clang rings out as the lorry's door comes free of its hinges and hits the tarmac. Those still in the vicinity turn to watch. One of the rescuers exclaims, and the expletive is repeated by her colleague. Jada moves to get a better view, but the bus lot have the same idea.

Again a curse from the cutters. Both men scramble clear of the lorry, the consternation clear on their faces.

The two police constables share a confused look and hurry over to assist, the black one talking into his radio on the way.

Fork lightning splits the sky; seven seconds later, a drumroll of thunder replies. The raindrops are now falling steadily.

Another shout, this one of fright, not alarm. Feeling butterflies in her gut, Jada breaks into a trot to get past the crowd. Now she's within ten yards of the crashed lorry. She points her camera at the wreckage.

The white policeman has a hold of his fellow officer, around the waist. He's barking orders: "Let go, sir!"

Is he trying to drag him clear?

A scream from the cabin. Blood sprays. Several bus passengers point, gasp or do both. The white cop bellows as he falls to the asphalt, lands on his back and hits his head. The crack turns Ada's stomach. More blood. More screams, not from the lorry – the black constable is now silent – but from the spectators.

"Someone help them!" an elderly man exclaims.

As if jolted out of a dream, Jada springs forward. But as she gets closer to the lorry, she sees. She sees why the black cop is quiet, why his legs are limp, why his torso is still leaning into the cabin, why there's so much blood. The trucker isn't a trucker anymore. His claret-stained face is a mask of spite, teeth and another man's flesh. His eyes are those of a shark, dead yet predatory. Briefly, the thing contemplates Jada, then returns to chewing on the policeman's right ear. The sound of tearing cartilage is nauseating.

Bells ring in Jada's ears as she stumbles backwards. Her vision clouds pink. She drops her camera. The wails of the bus passengers barely register… but then there's a screech.

It's a blood-curdling, almost feral bray of agony. Not shock or fear. Coming to her senses, Jada spins on her heel. Twenty yards away a jogger is on the ground. Atop her is an animal, but not an animal, a human, though it's attacking like a wolf, biting the throat, ripping and rending, growling and grunting, bloodthirsty, blood-driven.

Glass shatters. One of the closest queuing motorists is attempting to leave his car via the windscreen. He cuts his hands to ribbons in the process but is undeterred.

Time to go. Instinct takes over: head down, Jada sprints westwards.

Chapter 3 — Lena Adderley — 10:35

Bach's 'Air on a G String' gives way to Wiegenlied by Brahms, while the woman breathes in through her nose, out through her mouth.

The lorry crash is a headache, but nothing more. A negligible haul of Resurrex was on board, and its sole purpose was to be officially-presented to local authorities. That can wait now; Lena has bigger, more dangerous fish to fry.

Containing the situation is 'imperative', Gordon Villeneuve MP said. If they don't, his political career will be at stake, and he'll make sure he takes Evolve down with him. Also, he intimated in the brief telephone conversation with her that ended sixty seconds ago, the company's collapse would be 'the least of her worries'. To ensure he would face only disgrace rather than criminal charges, the up-and-coming Member of Parliament would stop at 'nothing', he threatened.

Except the slimy son-of-a-bitch isn't right about 'her worries'. As far as she's concerned, death at the hands of Villeneuve's army-thug buddies is a preferable alternative to the shame of Evolve's ruin. For Lena is no ordinary thirty-three year-old woman. She is heir to the Adderley family fortune, worth several billion. Moreover, with her father now crippled by dementia, she is responsible for the family's reputation, which barely survived the last scandal.

Don't be melodramatic, the voice of reason whispers in her head.

But she's not being melodramatic, because Evolve simply must survive. Being forced to break news of the chemical firm's demise to her father would destroy him. Due to his neurological disease, she would have to drop that same bombshell over and over; once a week, once a day, once every few hours or even minutes, eventually.

She can't let that happen to him. She owes everything to his hard work, from the expensive designer suit and shoes she wears, to the top class education and connections that gave her the strongest of starts in life. He may have been rash in business at times, but he's always wanted the best for his company and family. Most importantly, he's treated his wife and two daughters with the utmost care and respect.

What about the people of Mortborough, though? The citizens of Manchester, and England as a whole?

There's not a great deal she can do for them. Large quantities of Resurrex have already been distributed; the coming storm, which might even reach hurricane status, will carry the fertiliser across the whole of the northwest. Civilian deaths could number thousands, Villeneuve claimed, but Lena reckons he's just exaggerating to add pressure.

What if he's not? Perhaps we should be focussing on containing the lethal compound rather than concealing the company's and the Government's culpability.

No. Gordon Villeneuve has always been a liar; he'll use any angle he can to get what he wants. This time, he's over-played his hand, hammed-it-up a little too much. Zombies? The idea is risible; Resurrex was formulated to kill diseased plants then bring them back to life. Not humans.

I'm doing the right thing. Family comes first. I'm protecting the Adderley legacy and saving a foundering Tory government from another controversy.

Of course, there may be deaths. There will be a shred of truth in Villeneuve's words. Mortborough's townsfolk are likely doomed, because its surrounding fields have been treated for at least a fortnight now, and shutting down the factory/lab there won't reverse two weeks of fertilisation. Can Lena live with their deaths on her conscience?

Yes. I'll have to. Damage limitation is the focus now.

The heiress opens her eyes. She needs to squint, but only for a moment; it's not as bright outside the car as it was. She unplugs her earphones and hears rain pattering against the windscreen. There's a rumble as a HGV trundles past the lay-by in which Lena parked to take the video call from Villeneuve. She was already on her way to Manchester to meet with the mayor, so she's within twenty miles of Mortborough.

"Ignition," she says.

The Jaguar saloon's engine growls in response.

"Call Anderson."

A dialling tone begins and ends after four rings.

"Ms Adderley? Anderson receiving." The younger lady's voice is sweet, almost cute, her accent Scouse. Not what one would associate with an ex-Special Forces mercenary.

"Has our Right Honourable friend been in touch?"

"Yes, Ms Adderley."

"So you know?" Lena's tone is clipped, almost disinterested.

"Yeah. He told me to make it very clear that we're to assist you, but only for now. If you're unsuccessful, we go our own way."

"He's made that pretty clear to me already. Where are you?"

"Not far from town. I'm just calming things down. Remotely." Which means Anderson's using her hacking skills to kill all comms: sabotaging mobile networks, internet, landlines, et cetera. Soon, everyone in Mortborough will be unable to contact the outside world.

"I'll be there soon as well. I have a sat-phone, so keep yours handy too." Lena clears her throat. "Will Mr Lunt be joining us?"

"Yeah. We just spoke, an' he's en route."

"Okay. Good bye, Anderson."

"Bye, Ms Adderley."

Mr Lunt. *Harry.* Lena thought she'd left the former soldier in the past, but it appears that wound will be reopened. She can't argue with Villeneuve's rationale, however. Lunt is one of the best, a veteran of dozens of shadowy, Westminster-sanctioned operations over the last twenty years. When the Government puts its fingers in the wrong pies, when it becomes entangled with organised crime or corporate chicanery and cannot untangle itself, it uses tools like him. Although Anderson comes highly-recommended, she's a rookie compared to Lunt.

So, should she ring Lunt as well?

No, there's no need; Anderson is liaising with him, and the three of them will rendezvous in Mortborough. Despite herself, Lena checks her reflection in a compact mirror. It takes some effort not to apply lipstick, to leave her makeup bag in the glovebox. Her brown, bobbed hair is a touch unruly, but it will suffice. She's heading to her home town for business, not pleasure.

Time to go. She dons sunglasses and shifts the car into first gear. Indicating, she pulls onto the A-road and applies the accelerator with care. There are numerous speed cameras on this stretch, some of which link directly to Highway Police. Once she reaches Mortborough, she'll be practically immune to the law. Until then she needs to stay out of trouble. Traffic is light, the drizzle still negligible, though according to the Met Office, a storm is imminent.

Before long she's in Greater Manchester, and it's only just turned eleven o'clock. Visibility is deteriorating. Cloud cover is getting thicker by the minute. Her navigation system alerts her to congestion en route to her destination, so she exits the motorway earlier and travels the final five miles by country lane. Cows watch her black executive vehicle zip through the rain, but not many. They're thinner now, in both number and bulk. The yellow grass beneath their hooves is all but gone.

Another road closure means she has to enter Mortborough on the opposite side to the industrial estate where Evolve's HQ is situated. The company's de facto boss is not vexed by this diversion, though. It won't hurt to pass through the town; ascertaining the severity of the outbreak will help her determine the steps necessary to take. Dying fields surrender the land to retail parks, hypermarkets and offices as Lena leaves the countryside behind.

Thunder rolls. The rainfall worsens, making the Jag's windscreen wipers work harder. Their squeaking irritates the driver, who switches on the radio to listen to classical music. The clock displays 11:30, so Lena's making good time.

The B8102, normally fairly busy for a route of its size, is deserted. Trees used to line the street on the edge of town; the houses had gardens with flowers and shrubs. Not anymore. Slowing to 10mph, Lena scans the vehicles parked on both sides of the road. When she sees an otherwise immaculate convertible with a cracked passenger-side window, she stops her car in the middle of the road.

For a few heartbeats, Lena sits and watches. She watches the houses, the automobiles at the roadside. While doing so, she takes an inhaler from the bottle holder by the handbrake. One dose an hour, Aslam said, no more, no less. It's probably not necessary, but better to be safe than sorry.

She gets out and strolls to the closest pavement. The rain, heavier now, feels refreshing on her brow. There's no sign of foul play, no blood, no bodies. More unoccupied cars than one might expect at this time on a Monday, some parked a little haphazardly, and far less traffic, maybe. A faint smell of burning hangs in the air.

Villeneuve is so full of shit. Zombies!

A dog barks, and Lena's pulse quickens for a moment. From behind a van comes a friendly-looking Golden Retriever. The canine walks the human's way and is happy to have its damp ears stroked. A leash trails from its collar, the handle floating in a gutter puddle. *Not a stray.* It whines once, then espies a cat and gives chase.

Ridiculous as Villeneuve's tales of the crypt may be, something in Mortborough is amiss. Lena texts Anderson to supply her own coordinates and ascertain the agent's ETA. Anderson replies with: "Fifteen minutes - traffic". Sighing, the exec reopens her car door to escape the weather, but as she does so, a sound makes her stop. It's a child's or maybe a woman's shout. A panicked one at that, its source one of the neighbouring streets.

Lena licks her lips. Blinks rain from her eyes. Does she explore alone, or wait for her backup? Physical heroics have never been her forte, and she'll be of no use to Evolve if she gets hurt. Perhaps she should simply head straight for the factory and concentrate on covering-up the company's corner-cutting.

Fleetingly, she considers the hopelessness of her mission. With only two aides, she's expected to investigate the threat, calculate the chances of it being blamed on the Government, then somehow prevent such an outcome. Also, she's against the clock, for Villeneuve said she has limited time before the military step in. At that point, Lunt and Anderson will no longer be her allies. If she gets in their way, she'll be collateral damage.

Would Harry hurt me?

Again a scream. This time its meaning is clear: someone is in fear of their life.

Lena takes the satellite phone from a jacket pocket and places the call.

"I was wondering when you'd ring." Lunt's gravelly Scottish accent is comforting.

She strives to keep her tone casual. "How far away are you?"

"Ten minutes. Anderson sent me your location."

Glass smashes somewhere. A person not more than fifty yards away shouts, "Help!"

But they're not on this street, because Lena can't see anyone in either direction. "Hurry, please."

"You're not in your car?"

"No, I got out to —"

"— Get back in. Stay in your car. We'll come for you."

A third cry is cut short.

"Okay, but…" Lena's vocal chords freeze. Her brain struggles to comprehend the images relayed by her eyes.

"What is it? Lena?"

"I… it's…"

"Get. In. Your. Car."

It's coming for me. It came from that house's door. Now it's stumbling down the drive. And onto the street. It's bleeding from the mouth. Or is that… someone else's… it's someone else's blood. So much blood, drenching the boy's school shirt and tie. Now a woman, too. Her summer dress is more red than yellow.

And she's coming for me.

Chapter 4 — Harry Lunt — 11:40

The big man slams the 4x4 door shut, hard. He reopens it, then slams it again, this time letting out a grunt of rage as he does so. *That fuckin' condescendin' wee prick.*

But Gordon Villeneuve is paying Lunt's bills, effectively financing Mrs Lunt's cancer treatment. If they wait for the NHS to administer care, she'll probably die.

Therefore, her husband will remain professional and follow orders. Doing as he's told is second nature for Captain Harold Lunt (ret'd). As commanded, he parked a short distance outside Mortborough in order to arrive unseen. The rain won't bother him, for he's wearing tactical gear, but he can already feel sweat rolling down his spine. He's no stranger to hardship, however.

Locking his car door, he begins the short walk into the Greater Manchester suburb. After fifty yards on the bridleway, he's already regained his composure. He's a pro, an expert in self-mastery. He can disagree with his employer without rebelling, without letting it affect his performance.

The steady rainfall on his bald head gives him something sensory on which to focus. Soon enough, the dying woods around him give way to brown fields, and he can see two church spires above the mish-mash of housing estates, schools and shops. He sees four, no, five distinct plumes of smoke, as if the suburb is being blitzed. He sniffs. Diesel is burning somewhere; at least one of the fires is plastic. Perhaps it was caused by a lightning strike.

Two hundred yards from his parking spot – an abandoned farm half a mile north of his destination – Lunt reaches a canal. He crosses a bridge. He continues south down the footpath, which is now asphalted rather than a dirt track. Soon, the former soldier will be at the petrol station on the A5043.

Of course, if it were up to him, he would already be in town. He wanted to go in all guns blazing and rescue Lena. The politician insisted otherwise, arguing that Anderson is closer and would reach Lena quicker. Plus, like Lena, Anderson is expendable, but Lunt is valuable to Villeneuve.

Although several cars are parked at the Texaco, they are abandoned. One is still hooked up to a fuel pump, which makes Lunt frown. He has a bad feeling about this assignment. He isn't afraid – being tortured as a teenaged POW will either make or break a young man, and it was the making of him – but he reckons he'll have to ignore his moral compass for the next twenty-four hours. There will be civilians to silence, one way or another. A narrative to develop. Dark deeds will be committed for money, and the fact he'll spend his earnings keeping Maggie alive won't salve his conscience.

Plus, he's anxious for Lena, who isn't prone to exaggeration and sounded terrified on the phone. She and Lunt share history. Ancient history, maybe, but they had a thing eleven years ago, before he met his spouse. Guilt pangs as he realises he still has feelings for Grant Adderley's daughter, even with his wife's life on the line.

Shaking his head, he fishes the prescribed inhaler from a pocket of his combat trousers and takes his medicine. *Focus, ye daft bastard.* He circumnavigates the Texaco and tries to call Anderson again. No answer. Does he ignore his orders and make for the location Lena reported, or head straight to Evolve HQ? Essentially, it's a choice between a former lover and the woman to whom he swore vows. If he saves the former yet disappoints Villeneuve, Lunt won't get paid, and Maggie will wait months for her mastectomy. She doesn't have months.

He passes a retirement home on the right, then a row of shops on the left. He's still to see a living soul despite being in town for fifteen minutes. Plenty of cars, a couple of dogs and a fallen child's bicycle, yet no people. Twice he hears disturbances in the terraced houses he passes, but judging by the discarded syringes and vandalised bus stops, he's in a deprived area. The industrial park is less than half a mile away, so he presses on through the storm, marching as swiftly as he did during his days as a paratrooper. Lightning illuminates the gloomy sky, and thunder isn't far behind.

Reaching a junction, he checks the map app on his phone. Left will take him to the B8102, where Lena went silent. Right leads to his ultimate goal, the Evolve complex. He barely breaks stride before choosing the latter path. The smell of burning is getting stronger, but perhaps that's due to the wind.

With luck, he will solve the Government's problem while Anderson secures Lena, and they'll be done by tea time. Then Lunt can go home to Maggie, do the chores, walk

Bruce the German Shepherd and forget all about the Adderleys.

The next turn, a right, takes him out of the council estate and onto a high street. It also dispels any hopes he had for a swift, simple, in-and-out job. Halfway down the thoroughfare, nestled between a pawnbroker's and a betting shop, stands a police station. The Victorian building is on fire, as is one of the three squad cars parked in front. At least thirty other automobiles have been left in the middle of the road. Five of the vehicles are crashed in a row, nose to tail, with the front-most horizontally-positioned across the way. Shattered glass glitters in flickering headlights. Some of the larger slivers on the ground are stained red. Twenty yards up the high street is a bus, its engine smoking.

"Shit." Lunt takes his sat-phone and tries Anderson once more. "Pick up yer phone, woman."

Perhaps she can't. Perhaps she and Lena are —

A thump, as if a door's been closed. Standing his ground, the ex-soldier unzips his jacket and places his hand on the pistol in its concealed holster. As ordered, he left his heavier-duty weapons in the car.

Carefully he walks down the high street. He skirts patches of debris to avoid crunching it beneath his boots. The wind, picking up now, wafts smoke from the police station fire into his face. His watering eyes flicker from obstacle to hiding place; from near, to middle, to long distance; from alleyways to side streets.

Another noise. This one clearer: it's the musical tinkle of smashing glass. Suddenly, a cat darts across the road and up onto a shop awning. The feline hisses at the beauty salon from which it just escaped.

Sandwiched between a bakery and a vacant, boarded-up lot, 'Nailed It' is the one of the few buildings with a closed door. Teeth gritted, Lunt draws his suppressed Glock 21 but leaves the safety switch on. Villeneuve parting, codified words – "bid high only if absolutely necessary" – rattle around his brain. *Extreme prejudice in extreme situations only.* He creeps along the pavement. As he nears the nail bar, he angles his approach in order to get a decent view of the interior as early as possible.

The salon is deserted. Its interior is in disarray: two of the counters have been upended; a third is stained red. Colour charts, flyers and bank notes are strewn across the floor.

Not looters. The fuckers wouldae taken the cash.

Holding his gun low, Lunt pushes the door gently. It opens, and hinges creak. He waits for a reaction, but none comes, so he slips through the entrance. He uses peripheral vision to avoid stepping on anything while focussing on the frosted door in the shop's rear wall. Sniffing, he registers blood, urine and the acid of vomit. Silence reigns.

Now he sees the body. Hidden from view by a fallen advertising hoarding, the corpse is face down. It belongs a petite woman, with fine, straight, jet black hair; she's wearing a crop-top, denim miniskirt and flip-flops. Blood is pooling beneath her, under her head and shoulders. Stepping lightly for a man of his size, Lunt approaches. He squats to touch her carotid artery and gets nothing for his trouble but sticky, bloody fingers.

Sighing, he stands straight and continues towards the internal door. He doesn't have time for rescuing civvies, so he'll make sure this building is clear, then proceed to the industrial estate.

Bang! The door's opaque surface cracks. His handgun swings to bear. Bang! The crack spider-webs. Safety off. Smash! Shards are shaken loose and fall.

"I'm armed," the former captain rasps. "Come out wi' yer hands raised."

Another impact, and this time a bare arm and hand protrude through the frosted, jagged splinters. The sallow flesh is gouged red, the fingertips filthy.

"Stop! Or ahI *will* fire."

The door erupts, an avalanche of glass and raging human. The man is small, his face covered in blood and puke. His tattered, torn grey shirt snags on the door handle, and he staggers like a drunk. Coolly, Lunt compensates for the stumble and squeezes the Glock's trigger. Double taps. The noise is negligible. They are .45 ACP rounds firing at subsonic speeds, so there's no sonic boom. Both slugs hit centre-mass with a sound like meat being pounded. Blood spurts.

The crazed attacker reels away. He doesn't go down; in fact, he looks angry, inconvenienced by the 30g of metal in his chest.

Crazy bastard.

Lunt frowns and adjusts his aim to shoot the freak of nature between the eyes.

Down goes the man, landing on the woman's cadaver. His blood mingles with hers, fresh with congealed.

Cuffing sweat from his eyebrows, the gunman takes a moment to reflect. The dead guy wasn't wearing body armour. Nevertheless, with two 11mm holes through his heart, he stayed on his feet. *The bastard didnae even flinch!* A pragmatist at heart, Lunt isn't given to sweeping generalisations like 'that was impossible' or 'nobody could've survived that', but on this occasion, he is disconcerted.

Five seconds of deep breathing pass, and Lunt is relatively calm once more. He peers through the ruins of the staff-only exit and sees nothing of note. Just a desktop computer, a small safe, an overflowing bin, a mini-fridge.

Time tae go.

The ex-squaddie leaves the salon and is about to hurry in the direction of Evolve HQ when his sat-phone buzzes in his pocket. Anderson is calling him back. ~~Swallowing, Lunt~~He realises it could be bad news about Lena, so his hand trembles as he raises the device to his ear.

"Lunt."

"Ander— —ing. —nt, whe— a— —u?"

"Slow down, kid. Didnae catch any o' that."

"Hello?"

"Yes, Anderson, ah hear ye loud 'n' clear. Have ye found Ms Adderley?"

"I can't hear you, Lunt."

"Have. You. Found. Adderley?"

"Say again —"

The call ends, prompting a string of curses from the Scotsman.

Suddenly, Lunt recognises he's been talking too loudly. The thought of Lena in danger has wound him up; he's acting like a rookie, letting emotion override professionalism.

Perhaps I'm past it?

In any case, his outburst hasn't gone unnoticed.

Blundering towards him from the police station is a person. Its features are unclear, its gender unknown, because it's *on fucking fire*. Two more, a towering, dead-eyed brute of a man and a short, rotund woman, are coming from an off-licence Lunt passed five minutes ago. They're not ablaze, but they look maniacal, like the near-invincible psychopath in the salon. Now three blood-spattered mixed-race teens are exiting the broken-down bus. They move quicker than the others. Several shop windows on the strip burst open, too, birthing multiple scrambling, demonic fiends.

Simultaneously, ten snarling townsfolk dart towards the surrounded ~~newcomer~~<ins>Scotsman</ins>.

Chapter 5 — Connor Norman — 12:00

The boy frowns at his smartwatch. It was a gift from Dad for his 11th birthday, only two months ago; it should still work. Yet it says the time is midday, which can't be right. The light coming through the loft's window is too weak. Perhaps the sun has died, or something. Maybe that's why everyone's going crazy. Of course, he's considered the possibility that the sky is too cloudy. He's not an idiot. But Connor's never seen the sky this dark.

Thunder grumbles, making the child shiver. He's heard and seen plenty of lightning storms, though, so why is he so scared? So scared he barely tastes the inhaler's chemicals when he takes a puff. So scared he can't even climb out from under a carpet and peek through the skylight to see where the sun's gone. So scared he doesn't dare reach up to switch on the room's single ~~naked~~ lightbulb. So scared he would rather fight all the snakes in the world than go within ten feet of the attic hatch. So scared he's thinking about anything but the real world outside his hidey-hole.

Something's happened. Something — *no, dumb-ass, don't even think about it, 'cause if you don't think about it, it's not even really true.* That's what Kelsey Bryant in his class says. Of course, she-~~'s on the yellow table~~used to go to a special school, so she knows nothing.

He hears movement downstairs for the first time in at least half an hour. It's a shuffling sound, as if someone is moving furniture. A knock on wood. Then silence. Someone is here, in the house, someone who's not meant to be there. Or is it just Mum?

"Mum," Connor whispers without realising. It's no use anyway. Wherever she is, she can't hear him. Or maybe she can, but she hates him for some reason? No. She can't hear him because he's lost his voice, though e-~~E~~ven before it went, she didn't answer. Like Dad says, he's 'pissing in the wind'.

Despite himself, Connor smiles. His dad is funny; sometimes he swears when Mum's not around. They don't live together now,-~~though,~~ so Dad can say 'shit' and 'twat' whenever he wants.

What if Dad's dead now? What if Mum's dead? What if their only son can save them, bring them back to life — *okay, not bring them back to life. That's stupid.*

He could ring a doctor, at least. Then they can go back to looking after him, and he can stop worrying. But how's he going to do that if he can't even move a muscle?

The schoolboy steels himself. *I can just, like, take a look through the window, can't I? Just a really quick peep t' see what's going on, then duck back down.* The carpet is heavy; his arms feel even more puny than usual. With a heave, he casts the material aside and stands. His knees shake, but two steps later he's at the skylight.

It's not night time after all, though the clouds are almost black in places. Connor and his mum live at the top of a hill, so he can see for miles. There are half a dozen fires in sight, some fierce, some just smoking. *Is it terrorists, or somethin'? Why would they attack Mortborough~~, though~~?* It's a pointless little place, the sort ~~you~~one could live ten miles from and never know exists. *Or maybe the lightning is to blame?* As if to confirm, there's a flash over the town centre. Connor counts to four before thunder plays a drum solo in the heavens.

It's not the storm, dumb-ass. There's been tons o' storms in the past, 'n' none of 'em made the neighbours scream. They didn't make Mum stop talking 'n' start banging on the walls, either. A bit o' thunder 'n' lightnin' doesn't cause two car crashes on my tiny street alone.

But, he supposes, it has been a bad storm, the worst he can remember. That would explain the fires. Fires everywhere could make people scream, while the car accidents might be a coincidence. As for his mum, she's probably mentally ill. She takes tablets every day. When he first saw the pill bottle in the bathroom cabinet, he Googled the complicated name~~:~~ they're a~~A~~ntidepressants, apparently, which means she could 'go psycho' anytime. That's what Maz Khan, one of Connor's best mates, said, and he's the cleverest kid at school.

◄ *So what now?*

If Mum's insane, she'll need doctors and new medicine. Her new boyfriend Trent, who took Connor to watch United the other week, seems like a good man. He and Mum don't argue anywhere near as much as she did with Dad. Hopefully, he'll try to ring her, and when she doesn't answer, he'll come to investigate, in his new Mercedes.

More noise below. It's a tearing sound, but not that of clothes being ripped; it's more like when a dog is ~~playing~~ tugging with one of those rope and ball toys. When they're pretending to be wolves in the wild, but they're actually just playing.

Mum musta really lost the plot. Would she 'urt me? She's never even smacked me, not even when I smashed 'er new phone. She wasn't mental then, though, was she? Sometimes, when people really, properly go mental, they do 'orrible things. Like that guy who strangled everyone in his family then 'ung himself from a tree. One minute he's workin' at McDonald's, servin' burger 'n' chips. The next he's killing his wife and two sons.

Connor is conflicted. On one hand, he wants to be there for Mum, as she's always been there for him. On the other hand, she might be dangerous. He likes to think he's brave for his age, but even if he could bring himself to fight her, would he ~~stand a chance~~win? She's still six inches taller than him.

For a while, everything is quiet. The thunder is getting further away; there's no more shouting and fighting nearby. Connor checks his wrist again: it's only ten past twelve. Time is dragging more than it does during maths! Sighing, he swipes the watch's display to see if there's anything on the news about Mortborough. None of the apps are working. He has no Wi-Fi, no mobile data.

Shit. This is really serious. There's never been no Wi-Fi and no mobile data. I need t' do somethin'. I need to find out what's goin' on.

Connor summons every ounce of courage and tiptoes across the loft's laminate floor. Luckily, it was converted into a bedroom by Trent shortly after Christmas, because Mum's having a baby, so the floorboards aren't creaky. The boy drops to his hands and knees to turn the hatch's handle. Usually, he would simply let the door swing open then drop the ladder down. This time he allows the cover to hang for a moment while he peers through.

The landing light isn't switched on, and judging by the lack of illumination, it appears all of the bedroom doors are closed. Biting his lip, Connor swings the ladder into position. *Thank God Trent's kept it oiled. Dad would've never done that. Dad's never been into home improvements, but he's pretty good at Call of Battle.* Slowly, steadily, the child allows the ladder to slide out of its fixing. It extends quietly into the gloom, like a probe being dropped to the bottom of the ocean.

The dull thud outside elicits an involuntary whimper from Connor's hoarse throat. Worse still, the noise shocks him into dropping the ladder. With a metallic rattle, the rungs slip through his hands. The steel feet are tipped with rubber, but the impact <u>as they hit the floor</u> is deafening ~~even so~~<u>nonetheless</u>.

Vision swimming, the eleven year-old covers his mouth. The clang caused by his error is still reverberating in his ears. Ten agonising seconds pass. The only sound is that of his own pulse in his ears. There's no other reaction, ~~n.~~ No bangs on the walls, no staggering footsteps. *Are they, whoever they are, gone?*

Connor has a multitude of questions bouncing around his brain, like flies trapped against a table under a cup. He needs to calm down. Before Grandma <u>Josie</u> died, she ~~always~~ used to say 'less haste, more speed'. <u>She used to work on a farm, too, so she was always</u> busy. Rushing around doesn't actually make things happen faster; it simply means there's a greater risk of making mistakes. At the moment, he can't afford to make mistakes. The last one – dropping the ladder – could've cost him dear.

Connor places one foot on the ladder. Then another. And back to his left, then right. Before long, he's easing himself onto the varnished wood floor. He pauses, his ears straining. *I was super-quiet. Nobody 'eard me. Or did they? Maybe they're just, like, messin' with my 'ead —* "Get a grip, Connor," he ~~whispers to~~chides himself.

The house in which he stands seems suddenly alien to him. *Has Mum's bedroom door always been that colour?* It doesn't matter; what matters is finding his Mum and discovering what's happening. Tentatively, he pads across the floor towards the staircase. Before rounding the corner, he pauses. His heart hammers away in his head, in his chest.

What's that smell? Something mingin', like the bins at school.

He shifts his head just far enough to see around the wall and down the stairs. They are clear, so he begins to make his way down. Keeping to the left, because the right-hand side creaks. Halfway down he stops to listen. He hears nothing, but the ~~rotting~~disgusting stench is getting stronger.

The bottom of the stairway is just feet from the door. The hallway leads in the opposite direction, a left turn for Connor. Less hesitant now, he sticks his head over the banister to scan the hall.

Then the front door handle turns, and the kid freezes. He's caught between fear and hope: someone might be here to do him harm; or it might be his Mum. If it were a stranger, they would knock, wouldn't they? Even if they were bad guys, surely they wouldn't just open the door. They would try and trick their way in.

"Mum?" he croaks. *Mum would just walk in, ya dick. She wouldn't be pissin' about wi' the door 'andle.* This insight has come too late, however, because he's already opened his mouth. He squeezes his lips together, as if that will help.

The door stops rattling. Wondering if he has deterred the would-be intruders, Connor begins to edge forwards again. He's on the bottom stair when the uPVC door opens with such force that the handle embeds itself in the perpendicular wall. Connor looks at the crumbling plasterboard, then at the *thing* standing in the threshold. Then back at the battered door, and again at *it*.

Oh shit oh shit. What is that?

It used to be Ste Simkins from next door but one. Ste with the ill-tempered poodle, Ste who once accidentally popped Connor's ball with his car and apologised at length, Ste who took an Amazon parcel for Mum the other day. Ste was a gentle giant; now he's just a giant. One with blood and saliva crusting his beard, with a wound to his shoulder so deep the bone is showing. Large patches of his curly hair have been uprooted. His light blue shirt is stained and holed, and body hair sprouts through the tears. His eyes are glacial, his mouth slack. The fly in his denim shorts is unfastened, revealing yellow-stained boxers. Ste makes no sound but plenty of smell.

Yet the detail which disturbs Connor most is Ste's footwear. One foot is bare, the other fully socked and shod.

Oh shit oh no. I'm gonna shit meself. I'm gonna shit meself then get killed by Ste from number 12, who's gone so mental he's only wearing one shoe.

As Connor clambers back up the stairs, then the loft ladder, he hears the clump-slap, clump-slap, clump-slap of Ste's feet in pursuit.

Chapter 6 — Luke Norman — 12:15

Pinching the bridge of his nose, Luke half-smiles. "Can we please stop callin' 'em 'zombies'?"

"That's what they are, bro," Brad replies. "Just like in the movies."

"Exactly. The movies. This isn't a movie. Mary is *dead*. Like, really dead. This isn't make believe."

"Not surprised she's dead. You almost took 'er 'ead off with that fire extinguisher."

Luke feels nauseous again. The crack when he fractured Mary's skull keeps replaying in his mind. "That's not the point. Mary, plus Gurdeep 'n' Samantha from third, and Josh 'n' Riana from first, they were all real people. Who got sick. Not fucking zombies."

"Nah. Ya need t' change yer mindset, bro." Brad swigs water. "They ain't people no more."

"Okay, okay," Barry interjects. Unlike the other survivors, he's not content to sit in the break room; he paces and gesticulates. Annoyingly. "Let's concentrate on the bigger picture. We need to think outside the box —"

Brad snorts, while Luke can't help but grin. *Why am I amused? Everyone is dyin', 'n' we're barricaded in a buildin' that'll prob'ly be smashed to shit by those freaks soon, so why am I smilin' at anythin'?*

"What's funny?" Barry asks.

"'Bigger picture', 'think outside the box'," Brad scoffs. "Can't believe you corporate dudes still talk like that durin' the apocalypse."

"What's an 'apocalisp'?" says Tia.

"End of the world." They're the first words Geraint's uttered for the last hour. He's been behaving even more weirdly than usual, almost as if he's excited, not disturbed. "Excuse me." He hurries towards the toilet.

Tia blows a chewing bubble. "Why is it 'appenin', then? Like, why are people dyin', then comin' back to life?"

"Fuck knows," says Brad. "Some virus, or somethin'. Mary was pretty ill before she died, right?"

"Anyway," Barry continues, "speculating won't get us anywhere. As I was saying, are we fully prepared for the next attack?"

"No better or worse than for attacks one, two, three and four." Daphne, from HR, was based on Barry's floor. Her expensive beige trouser suit is now stained red, and her designer hairdo, coloured dark red, is awry. "What more can we do? Keep blocking up the door when they move the blockage. And repeat. Repeat and repeat until the Army, or whoever, comes."

"I'm not stayin'," declares Luke.

"Me neither." Brad stands. "We both got kids."

"You're not the only ones," Barry protests.

"Never said we were." Brad grabs the fire extinguisher and heads across the floor, taking care to avoid Cal's corpse and its accompanying blood stain. "What you do 'bout yours is *your* call. But it's been quiet fer a while now. So I'm gettin' some supplies." He points at the vending machine. "'N' I'm breakin' out. Gonna go get my ex-missus 'n' kid. Anyone who wants to come with is more than welcome."

Luke has no decision to make. It's not his habit to be judgmental, but he fails to understand why the other parents in the room aren't leaving to rescue their children too – now that the building is no longer surrounded by undead monsters.

"The zombies could be hidin'," Tia argues. "Like, waitin' for us to try 'n' get away before they come fer us again."

"That's not how it looked from the roof," Luke states simply.

Jimmy, Kendall, Safi, Aiden and Layla have said nothing thus far, but they were on the first floor. By all accounts, the bloodbath that ensued down there when Josh and Riana turned would traumatise them for life. Seven died, painfully and noisily. Seven.

Barry and Daphne, who are friends outside work, have been more vocal. A work experience kid named Danny was the only one to turn on their floor. He was in a wheelchair and was easy to subdue. The other forty-odd third floor people must've rung in sick, so they may well be terrorising somebody else by now.

Big Cal was Mary's only victim. A keen rugby player, he was strong enough to keep her occupied while Luke grabbed the fire extinguisher. His death, caused by a throat bite, was rapid yet horrific, but his sacrifice saved several lives. Taya, his Ghanaian team mate and mother of two, hasn't moved or spoken since Cal gurgled his last breath.

"Norman?" Brad touches his friend's shoulder. "You listening?"

Luke had zoned out; he barely even registered the din Brad made battering the chocolate vendor. "Yeah, sorry, what?" His hands are trembling.

"You good, bro? We ready to bounce?"

Images of Mary clinging to Cal like a middle-aged vampire torment him. The crazed faces of the freaks as they rammed the building's main doors, scoring forehead flesh on the cracked glass as they strained to get in. The animal stench as Taya soiled herself.

Connor. I need t' save Connor.

"I'm ready." Luke gives his head the briefest of wobbles and slowly stands. "I'll take the fire extinguisher."

"Okay." Brad finishes a peanut bar and hefts a chair leg. "No one else?"

Barry looks away and stammers something intelligible; Daphne shakes her head; Tia is tapping away at her phone, even though mobile data and Wi-Fi have been disabled for the last couple of hours; Geraint is still to return from the men's room. No one else responds.

"Remember," Brad says, "Keep an eye on the ones who got bit. They could… turn."

"And keep puffing on these." Luke rattles his inhaler and takes a hit himself.

Down to the basement the two friends go, gripping their makeshift weapons. The company car park's steel gates have taken a battering from the zombie attackers. CCTV footage, viewed in the security room on the ground floor, showed the way to be clear. Now they are looking through the grate, and they can see no threat. Still, Luke feels a trickle of unease in his gut as the shutter rises. Apart from a few scraps of clothing and dribbles of blood, there's no evidence of the dozens-strong horde that assaulted this entrance just forty minutes ago.

Out on the street, the rain has lessened to a fine drizzle. The smell of burning is all but gone. The wind makes the only sound; the thunderstorm has passed, for now. They will head to Brad's ex-partner Briony's house first, as it's only a quarter of a mile away.

The business park which houses Union Energy's head office has seen its fair share of destruction. Within a minute, the pair have passed three crashed cars, two abandoned vans and two corpses. The suit wearing man and cleaning-aproned woman are lying just twenty feet from each other, in the middle of the main road into the office district. The former appears uninjured but is cold and lifeless, while the latter's cause of death is obvious: he's been eviscerated.

A handful of crows scatter as Luke and Brad pass, only to resume pecking at the entrails when the humans are clear.

"Fuck, bro." Unlike his friend, Brad can't tear his gaze from the grisly scene. "This is grim."

"Yeah." Luke slows his pace a little; Brad's legs are shorter than his. "Gone from zero to full-on apocalypse in the time it takes to watch a football match. Next left?"

"Yup."

Once out of the business park, they aim for a roundabout, passing more abandoned vehicles and another couple of bodies. Taking a right, they leave the A road and enter the Shawbrook housing estate. The streets are narrower, with fewer vehicles. There are patches and trails of blood, plus one dismembered hand and, behind a garden hedge, a pair of slaughtered old people.

Brad is now pale. "Looks like the zombies defo came this way."

"I know, mate," Luke says, putting a hand on his friend's shoulder as they walk. "But there's loadsa houses 'ere. They can't *all* 'ave been raided."

"You sure?"

Luke follows the smaller man's stare. Every home they've passed in this avenue has been attacked. Front doors are ajar, windows holed or entirely shattered, lawns churned by the passage of feet. *It's like they're going door t' door. Like they're desperate t' murder as many o' these poor bastards as they can.* Obviously, Luke keeps such darker thoughts to himself. "We'll find LaRosa, mate. We'll find 'er."

"But what'll be left of 'er?"

Rather than offer another meaningless platitude, Luke stoops to grab an empty beer bottle, which he launches at a group of birds. The beasts flee, leaving the scavenged, blood-drenched, feather-flecked form of a toddler no older than two.

"Oh, fuck." Brad almost gives himself whiplash looking away. He's walking slowly now, his movements mechanical.

"Come on, Brad," Luke urges. *You've put a brave face on so far. Now isn't the time to go into shock.* Let's get a move on. We need to be as quick as we can, 'cause, you know, she might —"

"— Be dead?"

"No, still alive, I was gonna say. 'N' the quicker we get there..."

"Fuck... can't believe we're talkin' 'bout LaRosa bein'..." Suddenly, he's striding, almost trotting. "We need to dust, bro. I can't let LaRosa... I can't let that happen...

but she might already…" Now he's running, and Luke has to hurry to keep up.

They turn a corner and almost trip over a dead dog, which has a bloodied cat in its rigid jaws. "Nearly there!" Brad pants. "Down there, it's a shortcut."

The buildings on this close seem unscathed; perhaps the zombies rampaging through Shawbrook went in search of fatter pickings. Between two houses there's a ginnel, the entry of which is partially blocked by an overturned, half-emptied wheelie-bin. After hurdling the pile of takeaway trays and dog food tins, the two men surge down the alley. Left turn then right turn, onto Barber Crescent.

""Ere we are." Brad slows to a brisk walk. He wipes sweat from his hands onto his trousers. "I 'ope Briony's not pissed at me fer rollin' up unplanned."

Luke gives his friend a quizzical look. "Mate, I don't think she'll be bothered." He swaps the fire extinguisher to his left hand and flexes the fingers of his right.

"Oh, yeah. Good point. This is it. Number 15. Last time I was 'ere, 'er dad chased me… fuck." The flush on Brad's cheeks drains away.

"Mate, just 'cause the door's busted, doesn't mean they're not alright..." Luke holds the semi-detached's front yard gate open. "Just, slow down, mate, there could be, like…"

The shorter man takes the crazy paving path in six brisk strides, with his friend close behind. Into the house Brad flies, shouting, "LaRosa! LaRosa, where you at?"

The only reply is a gust of wind from the rear of the property, where the back door gapes wide. A fly screen flaps in the draft; wind chimes jangle a melancholy tune.

"LaRosa!" Brad pounds his way up the stairs. "LaRosa! Where you at, kid?"

The downstairs hasn't been properly explored, so Luke opens a pantry, then a ground floor toilet. Both are empty. And there's a smell here that he doesn't like, one that makes his heart sink and his stomach contort. *Brad'll be devastated. Then it'll be* my *turn. Connor's house'll 'ave the same awful stink, and he'll be* —

On the first floor: "LaRosa, there you are!"

Thank fuck for that.

"LaRosa, what you doin', kid? What you got there… oh fuck… Luke… oh fuck… nooooooo!"

The scream makes ice of Luke's blood. Almost choking on his own dread, he takes the stairs two at a time.

"No, LaRosa… no, kid, that's naughty, you can't do that t' Mummy, you gotta…"

The girl's daddy, motionless in the bathroom doorway, has dropped his chair leg cosh. He stands with his hands on his head as though threatened by a bank robber. His speech garbles as he begins to sob.

Suddenly, something leaps onto him; it moves like a chimp yet snuffles like a pig. Brad reacts too slowly, but Luke's directly behind him. The taller of the two catches the toddler by the arm as she lands on her dad.

Undead LaRosa's incisors snap shut millimetres shy of Brad's neck. She's strong, a ball of pure fury. She almost manages to clamp her glistening red teeth on Luke's wrist, but somehow he and Brad restrain her.

The latter bear-hugs his daughter from behind; she struggles, but her arms are pinned to her sides.

Luke grabs the fire extinguisher he just dropped and raises it high.

"No!" Brad spits. "We might be able to save 'er."

His friend shakes his head. His eye is caught by the black woman's carcass on the floor: Briony. Her breasts are bare, half-chewed away. Yellow lumps of body fat mottle the crimson ruin of her bosom. The girl she birthed a few short years ago was in the process of eating her own mother. "She's gone, Brad. Sorry, mate, but she's gone. They're both gone.

Chapter 7 — Harry Lunt — 12:40

Battered but not bitten, the former SAS man jogs back from his car, heading straight to Lena's last known location. He needed more firepower. Much more ammunition. With only his pistol, he barely escaped the attack on the high street. A lesser soldier would've succumbed, but he made every shot count. Twice he was knocked over, and twice he blasted the beasts away just as they were about to savage his face. *They're quick, these fuckers. Strong, too. Like humans on steroids. Let's see how they like the semi-automatic combat shotgun, but.*

Lunt lost his satellite phone during the fight. He managed to retain his personal mobile, which is effectively useless thanks to Anderson's communication wizardry. Therefore, he'll need to find another way of locating Lena. The mission is on the back-burner for the time being. He'll do his best to satisfy Villeneuve, but first he needs to save his ex-lover from the gruesome aberrations prowling the streets of Mortborough.

On his way to Walker Road, the B8102, he encountered two zombies. One was coming out of a large detached house, the other on a street corner. Conserving his big gun's ammunition, he headshotted both with his Glock.

Minimum fuss, maximum results. *Just like auld Sergeant Kilbride taught me.*

A doleful, shaggy dog aside, Walker Road is deserted. Lunt lets the mutt nuzzle his hand. "Poor wee lad. Dinnae think yer owner's coming home."

Ms Adderley's Jaguar saloon is parked in the middle of the thoroughfare. The car won't start, so she must still have the key, wherever she is. There's no sign of a struggle in the vicinity. Of course, if she were attacked by the same monsters that went for Lunt earlier, there wouldn't be a struggle. Just a slaughter. "Fucksake, Lena," he mutters, "where did ye go?"

Shaking his head, the big man takes his inhaler from a pocket and puffs once. He begins to walk towards the town centre. By accident he kicks a can, which is full so catches his attention. Then he sees blood. *Shit.* There's not much, though, just a few drops. Not enough to come to any conclusion. Plus, it could be anybody's. Lunt stoops and touches the liquid; it's fairly fresh. Six yards away, there are more droplets, and four yards after that, another scarlet dribble. In any case, the clues lead in the direction he was already planning to take, so he may as well follow them.

After a single right turn, the trail goes cold. "Fucksake. What a shower o' shite." Maybe Lena will have to look after herself.

In the distance, thunder mumbles, but it's at least five miles away. The rain has all but stopped. It feels fresher now, the air less charged; one could almost forget that bloodthirsty subhumans are murdering and eating each other. Not for the first time, Lunt wonders what's happened in this once mundane, nondescript town.

He's on his way down the next avenue when a familiar sound stops him in his tracks. Straight away he recognises it: it's an automatic weapon, a submachine gun. The gunshots are in steady bursts, so the shooter's either an amateur, or they're in trouble.

Lunt changes course, bearing towards the racket. Into a back alley he dashes. That's where he sees Anderson, who, with her back to a brick wall dead end, is facing down a dozen zombies. The same number are already down. She's still firing. Stopping smartly, he avoids running into a stray round. "Hey, fuckers!" Lunt waves his arms.

Like puppets having their strings jerked, the freaks turn towards him. Half begin to shamble his way, while the remainder continue to menace Anderson. But he's bought her a little more time, and, together, they clear the alleyway of undead. The clumsy monsters spasm and quiver as head shots blow their brains and skulls against their fellow zombies, before falling to the cobbles. Blood seeps into puddles. Ragged clothing stirs in the wind.

Lunt reloads the pistol. He left the SPAS-12 tactical shotgun strapped to his back, saving it for direr straits. "Saved yer arse."

"Nope. I was doin' just fine." Anderson grins, but her face is pale.

"Pile o' metal jackets around ye says otherwise, hen." He nods at the bullet casings in the mud. "Go for the head, every time."

"I know. I'm not fucking retarded. They were just gettin' too close, so I was slowin' 'em down."

"Fair dues. Bit of a shit-storm this, eh?"

"Yep."

Lunt helps to collect the spent Heckler & Koch MP5 cartridges on the ground. "Where's Lena?"

"Fuck knows." Anderson's voice is tight. She walks past the big fellow and back onto the street. "I've never killed civvies before."

"These aren't civvies, so don't worry 'bout it. They're somethin' else now. Ye no' tried ringing her on yer sat-phone?"

"I did speak to her. She was bein' chased. But my phone's been malfunctioning since then. Fuckin' cheap-ass government equipment. Where we goin'?"

"To the target area, Evolve HQ. Hopefully we'll come across Lena en route. Presumably she's goin' that way." *If she's still alive.*

"If she's still alive. Sorry, I know you an' her... but just bein' realistic."

"She'll be fine." Lunt takes a left, onto a larger, broader road, one with a pub and a convenience shop about fifty yards away. As ever, abandoned cars are commonplace.

Anderson stops at the junction. "Shouldn't we just, like, get outta here? Call in the cavalry? I know we're good, Lunt, but you've seen 'em. These... things. You're just walkin' along, no one around, then *bam*! You're surrounded."

"We've a mission tae complete." *'N' a woman tae save.* "But yer right. We cannae be on foot. Need tae find a vehicle."

"Whose fuckin' idea was it, anyway, to park outside town?" Anderson is already checking the saloons, hatchbacks and SUVs jamming up Montserrat Drive.

"Straight from the top." Lunt focuses on automobiles more than two years old, as they won't be secured by biometric scanners. "Ah can kinda see the sense in it, fer covert jobs. Here we go. 1995, VW Golf GTi. Practically a vintage." He opens the solid door. "Nice 'n' sturdy, too. Shit, no keys."

"Hotwire?"

"Havnae done that in years. You?"

"I've seen it done in old movies."

"Great." Lunt leans under the steering wheel and pulls away the plastic panel covering the ignition. "Like ridin' a bike," he says. Connecting two wires, he's rewarded by the growl of the diesel engine. "Lift off."

"Well done." She climbs into the passenger seat. "You're not bad for an old bloke."

"Less o' the 'old', hen." He slips the Golf into first gear, then manoeuvres past a couple of the more wildly parked vehicles.

A moment later, they're clear of the queue. Lunt checks the map saved on his phone, quickly memorising the way to the industrial estate. Even so, he keeps glancing out of the windows to both sides, keeps checking his mirrors.

"You wanna look for her, don't you?" Anderson is appraising her reflection in the sun visor mirror. Despite the ruckus in the alleyway, she looks immaculate: her bleached blonde hair neat, her makeup still perfect.

"Look for who, hen?"

"Fuck off, Lunt. I know ya better than that. Listen, Evolve HQ's not goin' anywhere, is it? And with the odds we're facin', the bosses can hardly blame us if we're a bit delayed, can they?"

"What ye suggestin'?"

"We take a detour. Try an' find Lena. If I was her, I'd have headed for the park, the big one near the Tesco Superstore. Parks, especially on a Monday, are quiet. Less people about equals less zombies. Lena's smart. That's where she'll have gone."

"Good thinkin'." Lunt does a u-turn at a traffic light, sending a flock of birds scattering. "Why so charitable all of a sudden?"

"What you talkin' about?"

"Sentimental, I mean. I've never known ye tae jeopardise a mission fer a helpless civilian."

"People change." Anderson turns to look out of the window, at a deserted children's outdoor jungle gym and a library.

"Aye? Anyone ah know?" Lunt smiles conspiratorially.

"No… nothin' like that. Just… I was on a job recently… standard terrorist cell infil. Got a call sayin' a good mate was ill. But I was in deep… I thought she'd pull through…"

"She didnae?"

"No."

"Same thing happened wi' m' ma, then m' da. Shouldae learnt m' lesson first time, ah guess. Two sisters havnae spoken tae me since."

"That's the thing with this line of work."

"Aye."

They travel in silence for half a mile, passing burnt-out cars, stray dogs, several corpses and at least fifty zombies. When the fiends see the hatchback, they scramble away from their current meals and follow the passing vehicle. They're never swift enough, of course, but their speed, stamina and single-mindedness is frightening.

"Here we are." Lunt runs a red light and turns into the parking lot. Covering six hundred acres, Warrencroft

Country Park features a boating lake, seasonal funfair, golf course, petting zoo, numerous sports fields and playgrounds and, curiously, a castle. There's plenty of open space, a plethora of hiding places.

Anderson frowns. "You're not stoppin', are ya?"

"No." Lunt steers towards a service road. "This road runs right through the middle. There's a big auld castle in the centre."

"A *castle?*"

"Aye. Not authentic medieval, but. Only wee. The owner was some crazy 1800s dude who was intae the Middle Ages. Solid walls, no' many entrances, a good view o' the surroundin' area. Great place tae hole up, 'n' Lena knows it well."

The road turns a blind corner, and the fields give way to woods. It's dimmer under the trees. Not as gloomy as it would be if the sycamores weren't stripped of their leaves, though. Another twist takes them back into the open, where Lunt slams on the brakes. "Shit."

The way ahead is clogged by bodies. Male and female, they share two common features: they are elderly; they wear numbered bibs.

"Some kinda charity thing for old folks?" Anderson wonders. "Just drive over 'em."

"Cannae do that!" Lunt grimaces. "Some of 'em could still be alive."

"Doubt it. There's a lotta blood."

She's right. The gravel path is still wet from the storm, but the red patches are unmistakable. The white vests and polyester shorts of the competitors are filthy with soil and gore.

"Still, I'll drive around."

Which turns out to be a terrible idea, for the ground to either side of the path is waterlogged and boggy. The Volkswagen sticks in the mire, its tyres spinning and engine whining.

Lunt barely manages to reverse the car back onto the road. He climbs out and gives the prone figures a cursory inspection. *They all* look *dead, don't they?* "Looks like we're squashing power-walkers."

Anderson rolls her eyes. "Shoulda just listened to me in the first place."

Grimacing, the driver eases the automobile over the first dead body. It sounds as if he's pushing a wheelbarrow over twigs. "Jesus wept."

He's moved no more than five yards when he begins to feel added resistance, as if he's driving in the mud again.

"What's up?" says Anderson. "Should that be happening?"

"Dunno. Never driven over human corpses before, funnily enough."

After leaning out of the car to take a look, Anderson recoils. She winds the window back up and says, "Speed up."

"What's wrong?"

"Just drive."

Lunt tries, but the Golf won't budge. "What is it?"

"Those old dead people. They're not dead anymore."

After glancing at his wing mirror, Lunt gulps. Undead hands are pulling at the wheels, ripping them out of position, fixing the car in place. Now some of those ahead are rising to their feet. Swarms of flies disband as carrion reanimates. Drooling and dripping blood, faster and stronger than they've been for decades, dozens of pensioners converge on the disabled car.

Chapter 8 — Connor Norman — 13:20

Back where I started. What a dumb-ass.

But who can blame him? Ste from next door but one is a psychopath; Connor was going to be his next victim. Luckily, the child managed to wind up the loft ladder in time, so he won't end up slaughtered like everyone else. Has Ste killed Mum? Or has something else happened to her? After all, there seems to be trouble all over town, what with the fires, sirens, car crashes.

Perhaps there's some sort of major catastrophe, a terrorist attack for example, and Ste is just taking advantage. Connor watched a movie like that once. Set during a war, amidst the bombing raids and amphibious assaults, a serial killer was on the loose. The emergency services were too distracted to catch the criminal, who struck again and again…

Except that was just a movie, wasn't it? Things that bad don't happen in real life.

Is Ste just sick? He could need help; maybe a doctor or family could come around and try to calm him down. Once they've treated that gruesome cut on his shoulder, they could persuade him to wear both shoes.

No, you idiot, there's no helping Ste. He's a zombie, like the ones in 'From Beyond the Grave' on XBox.

Thinking like that isn't useful, though. There are no adults around – apart from Ste, who's still lumbering around directly below – so Connor has to be more mature. He needs to come up with a plan, whether that entails staying put until a real grown-up arrives, or fleeing his home and looking for somewhere else to stay.

At least he's safe up here in the attic. He has time to think, time to prepare, a bit like when he was revising for the SATs. He's hungry and thirsty, but he reckons he can survive for a few hours without sustenance. By the time he begins to starve, the police or army will come, and —

A bang downstairs: the front door. *Ste prob'ly didn't shut it behind 'imself, did he?* Footsteps, these ones normal, not uneven like Ste's, echo through the house. The stairs creak, and it sounds like when Trent comes up, not when Mum comes up, so it's someone heavy. There's not just one person, either. Two, no, three people are on the way up to the first floor.

Am I saved?

Probably not, because if they were friendly, they would shout a greeting. Now there are four people, including Ste, pacing the landing and bedrooms.

A second bang, this time against the loft hatch, catapults Connor's heart into his mouth. They can't know he's up there, though, can they? Ste hasn't said a word, but perhaps he's signalling to the newcomers, pointing at their quarry's location. Again, there's a thump, and the trapdoor shifts slightly.

I need t' get out. I need t' get out now.

Pulse throbbing in his ears, the boy stands. He can smell something foul now; it reminds him of when the drains were blocked. Over to the skylight he creeps. Reaching as high as his five foot frame will allow, he opens the window. He strains to keep it from squeaking as it yawns. The fresh air is almost delicious, the wind pleasant on his clammy brow.

But 'ow do I actually get out?

Glancing around, Connor spots an old chair that will take his weight. Once, a million years ago, his mother shaved his head while he was sat on that chair. He had head lice, and the prescribed shampoos weren't working. Tears well in his eyes. He wipes them away.

The attic hatch is hit for a third time. Dust stirs, making Connor squint.

Back across the floorboards he pads. He grabs the rudimentary stepladder, takes it and places it beneath the hole in the ceiling, climbs into place and, using all of his strength, drags himself onto the roof. As he pushes upwards, the chair tumbles over. Someone in the house must hear, as there's a sudden commotion and, in quick succession, another three bumps against the trapdoor.

Taking care not to slip on the rain-sodden roof tiles, Connor edges his way down to the edge overlooking his back garden. The lawn is clear of intruders. As is the patio. From this vantage point, however, he can't see the narrow passageway that leads past the open side of his semi-detached house. The drop is too far for him to jump to the ground, so he follows the gutter away from the passage, towards the shed. Twice he nearly slips, but the grips on his new trainers save him on both occasions.

The outhouse roof is about eight feet below him. Dropping such a distance will hurt his ankles, and he won't be able to roll when he lands, like they do on TV. But he has no other choice. For a moment he pauses. Scrutinising the closest gardens, he sees no threat, not yet. His next door neighbours, a childless couple in their forties named Naz and Jenny Amin, are away on holiday.

Just do it, ya soft-arse.

Connor holds his breath and steps out into the void. His plummet is short, his landing surprisingly pain-free. Suddenly buzzing with adrenaline and pride, he crosses the shed's asphalt and drops into next door's back garden. This time he can break his fall with a forward roll-over, which he completes with aplomb. The grass is overgrown, the ground soft and yielding. Fortunately, he didn't land on one of the piles of paving slabs Naz has been talking about laying for the last year.

This is easy! It's like I'm a commando, or somethin' —

Glass smashes in the Amins' house. Stumbling footsteps, the squeal of a shoe sole on linoleum. Gasping, Connor springs forward. He vaults the fence and lands in the alley between number 14 and number 12. Without even glancing to his left or right, he repeats the trick to enter Ste's property.

Ste. He'll be even more angry if he realises I'm sneakin' 'round his water features 'n' gnomes. Or maybe he won't care.

So he continues his jaunt, from garden to garden, hurdling fences and hedges, snagging splinters and scratching himself on brambles, dodging ponds and swerving past greenhouses, slipping on wet turf, tripping on plant pots. He thinks he hears enemies in pursuit, but he doesn't wait to find out.

He continues until he reaches 2 Simister Walk, home to a reclusive elderly man known only as Bud. The first house on this side of the street, it's bordered to the rear and side by hedgerows too thick and high for Connor to conquer. The ginnel leading to the front of the property is gated, and said gate is bolted and padlocked. Briefly, he jangles its chain in despair; then he remembers he needs to be quiet. Scaling the obstruction is out of the question, too, as it's topped by razor wire.

The youngster mops his forehead and neck, which are slick with sweat. The thunder and lightning have ceased, but the air is still oppressively humid. Thinking of his next move makes him perspire more. He has only two options. One, he can head back the way he came and risk coming face-to-face with the zombies in his wake. Two: breaking into number 2, avoiding any monsters inside, and escaping via the front door.

A rattle from the fence he's just climbed makes the decision for him. Bud's back door is pushed to, with its key in the inside lock. After slipping inside, Connor secures the exit behind him. He cuts through a small yet meticulously-clean kitchen, grabbing a loaf of bread on the way. He finds himself in a hallway, where he almost stumbles over Bud. The old fellow is sprawled, face down, in a smear of blood on the old-fashioned carpet. The nape of his neck has been mauled so badly that one of the vertebrae is exposed. A reek of shit and worse hangs heavy in the corridor.

Don't be sick, don't be sick, don't be sick, don't —

The boy's stomach evacuates its contents, covering Bud's left arm and shoulder in vomit. "Oh god, Bud," he whispers, his already-tender throat burning with bile. "I'm so sorry." Feeling faint, Connor steadies himself against an artexed corridor wall.

A crash against the back door refocuses his thoughts. *Pull yerself together, asshole.* He skirts the gory, puke-soiled corpse and dashes for the front door. Which is locked. *Where's the damn key? Maybe Bud's got it.* Gingerly he kneels by the dead man. He slips one hand under the man's right leg to check his pocket. It's empty. His heart soars when he feels cold metal in the left-hand trouser pocket, but the key is attached to an MG fob. He keeps the car key, though, because it could come in useful.

Movement from the end of the hall seizes his attention. The light from the tall window beside the front door is blocked momentarily, then unblocked, then blocked once more. Suddenly the letterbox opens; a dark-skinned hand appears, the spindly fingers flexing and probing. Without looking away from the appendage, Connor opens a door opposite the kitchen's.

Bud's lounge is as tidy as the rest of the house. Compared to the hallway, it's brightly-lit, as the south-facing bay window is wide and tall. Connor doesn't make the mistake of entering the room, though, because he can see figures outside. One, a tall man in a police uniform, is motionless save for a slight sway from the hips. He doesn't seem to be concerned about the ghastly hole in his cheek. The second zombie isn't quite as still; the teenaged girl waves one handless arm in the air as if hailing a bus.

In the kitchen, a window smashes. Glass crunches. A dragging sound is followed by a bump.

They're in.

Stifling a whimper, Connor leaves the living room and tries another ground floor door. It opens into an integral garage, and there it is: a racing green sports car that, despite being beautifully maintained, looks about fifty years old. By its side there is a petrol can, which feels full.

MG. This is my ticket outta 'ere. I've played enough drivin' simulators to do it, 'n' Dad used t' let me drive around the farmyard when we stayed at Gran 'n' then Grandad's farm. 'Ow 'ard can it be?

The classic car won't be DNA scan secured, not according to Dad, who said only new cars feature advanced security measures. Connor bolts the garage's internal door at the top and the bottom. He glances at the mechanically-operated shuttered exit: it'll be noisy when it opens. Worse still, it won't be quick. *I'll just start the car and ram my way out.*

Licking his lips, Connor inserts the key into the automobile's door lock. It turns smoothly. He grabs the jerry can and puts it in the boot, then slips into the driver's seat and attempts to get the key in the ignition. After a moment of fiddling, he has success. He wipes sweaty palms on his shorts, says a brief prayer, moves his chair forward, then switches on the power. The antique vehicle responds instantly, purring like a friendly lion.

Yes! Laters, freaks.

Connor steps on the gas. The engine revs, but the wheels don't move.

Oh, yeah.

He levers the handbrake off and presses the accelerator again. Once more, the car growls; again, it remains still.

Shit. I need t' change gears, press a clutch, or somethin', right? But 'ow does that work?

A minute passes as he paddles away at the pedals and wrestles with the gearstick. The MG's making a lot of noise, but it's going nowhere. Said racket is attracting attention, too. The garage's internal door and its external shutters are being battered by flesh-hungry zombies. Soon, they'll break through, and Connor will end up like Bud. Or Ste.

He's pouring with sweat now. Pushing the accelerator isn't working, and he can't hear himself think. He just needs a moment to think, a few seconds of quiet.

Such silence is unattainable, however. The zombies assaulting the garage's two entrances are making an almighty din. Although the robust internal door isn't budging, the vehicular exit looks ready to give way.

I need another plan. Or I'm gonna die.

Then Connor remembers the fuel in the trunk.

Chapter 9 — Jada Blakowska — 13:50

She wipes mascara from salty eyes. It's time.

No, it's not! Are you mental? Those ugly bastards will be back soon, an' then you'll be screwed.

She needs to be brave and strong, just as Mum taught her when Dad got ill. Her parents didn't raise a weak, feeble female. Therefore, she takes one last look through the disused warehouse's cracked, grimy window and retraces her steps. Back through the staff room with its used plastic cups on formica tables. Along a corridor, past the large double doors bearing the legend 'DISPATCH'. And finally, after a few deep breaths, into the women's bathroom.

The body is still in place. Lay on his side, the deceased man hasn't moved. He's chubby, scruffy and was probably rosy-cheeked before he died. Presumably, he had the same idea as Jada, thinking the derelict distribution site would make a good hiding place. He was right, it seems. The rioters didn't kill him; there's no sign of foul play. A few red spots are on the tile closest to his face, so he probably collapsed and coughed up blood. Maybe he had a heart attack from the stress and exertion of being chased by cannibals.

I'm pretty close to a coronary myself, to be fair.

Using meditation techniques she learnt practising yoga, Jada strives to calm herself. She's leaving the warehouse. She'll be in more danger, which should make her panic, when she actually needs to be cooler than ever. The journey from the dual carriageway, on foot, was two hours of hell. Whatever she encounters next can't be any worse.

Therefore, she's leaving the sanctuary offered by Speedster's Manchester depot and venturing outside. Any moment now, she'll squeeze back through the ladies room's broken window, descend the drain pipe and hit the ground running.

Just another a minute to prepare. One more minute.

Fuck that. It's time.

Jaw set, the journalist pushes the cubicle door wide and steps onto the toilet rim, then onto the cistern. She clambers through the window, taking care not to cut herself. Thanking the Lord for a childhood of tree climbing and fence jumping, she shimmies down the waste chute and drops three feet. As soon as she hits the asphalt, she darts behind a large bin.

Breathe in for five, out for seven. In for five, out for seven.

It stinks behind the dumpster, and she shouldn't stay in one place for too long, as so many found to their cost on the A9015 earlier. So Jada risks a peek around the side of the container: she sees no threat.

The air is humid and warm. Not as stifling as it was last time she was outside, though. The skies aren't as dark, either, and she hasn't heard thunder for a while.

The warehouse is on the edge of Mortborough, on the opposite side of town to Evolve's head office. Nearby, a right-hand turn at a junction fifty yards away, there are eight high-rise flats, which Jada plans to avoid. Tower blocks mean lots of people packed together, as they were in the traffic jam on the way to Manchester. She needs to keep away from crowds. They're either a large target for the lunatic predators on the loose, or they're the lunatic predators themselves.

This morning, the A-road was a perfect storm of both. Hundreds of motorists. Dozens of vicious attackers. Biting, being bitten. Feeding, being consumed. Man on man, woman on man, man on woman, woman on woman. Adult on child...

She shakes the waking nightmare from her mind. *Need to make a move.* At times, over the last couple of hours in the Speedster building, she's been angry. She craved answers – knowing why ordinary Mancunians were gorging on man-flesh would be a start – and she intended to share said knowledge with the world at large. Becoming convinced that Evolve plc are somehow involved, she intended to head across Mortborough to investigate their factory.

Now that she's outside, she feels differently. With the smell of burning in her nostrils and the occasional faraway human yell in her ears, she's less inclined to curiosity. Her first priority is becoming increasingly obvious. She needs to find a way out of this town, promptly, before she ends up as some psycho's lunch.

She goes left at the intersection. Highgate Road. She knows it well, having once had a boyfriend whose drug dealer lived in one of the terraced houses, which are as impoverished as she remembers. Many of the windows and doors are covered by steel panels. Used condoms, empty nitrous oxide canisters and broken bottles line the gutters.

A zombie apocalypse might improve the area.

"Don't be a dick," she mutters to herself. The undead are used for shock value by lazy writers and filmmakers. Something strange is happening in Mortborough, but there will be a scientific, plausible explanation, not one involving the rise of the dead.

And it's something to do with those bastards Evolve...

There's a car mechanic's around the next corner, and hopefully it's still trading. If she can break in, she can steal keys for one of the second-hand cars on sale. Thankfully, her parents and teenaged brother are visiting Poland, so she doesn't have to worry about finding them.

She's about to take a right onto McLeod Road when a nearby scream stops her dead. It's a woman or a child, perhaps. They sound scared, terrified even.

Gritting her teeth, Jada bobs her head around the wall of the corner house. The next street is as empty as those she's already walked. A couple of cars, burnt-out shells by this point, are in the middle of the road. Fifty yards away lies Mortborough MOT's. Its erroneous grammar used to bother Jada; now she's pleased to see the vehicle repair shop and the budget cars in front. Another cry, this one of pain and no more than two streets away, spurs her onward.

The business's gates are wide open. A cursory glance through the railings to either side of the gateway reveals no occupants. Still, her legs shake as she crosses the forecourt. Her ears strain for any sign of danger, the slightest footfall or movement. The crazies don't talk to each other, but they're far from quiet. They snarl, rasp and gurgle, and in Jada's limited experience, they become even louder when near potential prey.

No one home, thank fuck.

The reporter looks through the workshop's office window. It's dark inside, but she can see the cabinet on the back wall, the type where car keys hang from small hooks. On the floor are two shapes. Two large, dark, unmoving masses. A hand to her mouth, Jada pauses, conflicted. On one hand, she needs transport; surviving the massacre on the dual carriageway was a fluke, nothing more. On the other hand, she's scared, to put it mildly.

The shop is small, cluttered with piles of tyres and a variety of car accessories. If one of the dead people on the ground rises to their feet, Jada will be within feet of death.

Stop bein' a pussy and get on with it.

The door handle is sticky with blood. Wincing, she pulls it down and pushes the door open. A smell of oil greets her, but it's adulterated by the sickly sweetness of blood. The two bodies remain prone, even when she creeps past them to get behind the counter. Inevitably, her gaze lingers on the butchered pair.

The closest to the door, a youth in shorts and baggy t-shirt, is on his back. His face is sheeted claret, especially around the mouth. His afro hair is matted too, and something else glistens amidst the curls. *Ugh, is that brain?* The other man wears mechanic's overalls; he still grasps a monkey wrench and lies face down in his own vital fluids.

Thankfully, the cabinet is unlocked. Rather than sift through the seven keys in the shop, she takes them all, looping their keyrings onto her left forefinger. Again she tiptoes through the workshop, but a movement in her peripheral vision, something outside, distracts her. She treads in something wet. Her foot slides. As a result, she kicks an empty jerry can.

Movement again. This time closer, much closer.

Did the repair guy's fingers twitch?

No. He's bled so much he must be entirely exsanguinated. There's no way he's still alive.

His fingers definitely moved. Leg it!

No, she needs to take her time, for rushing will only draw attention. Besides, what did she see outside? She will go slowly, open the front door a crack, spy through the opening for a moment, then head for the row of second-hand cars. Every step calculated, every manoeuvre planned and considered. Certainly no hollering or sobbing, like so many – including Jada – on the Manchester Parkway a couple of hours ago.

The mechanic's hand, the one not holding the tool, moves. There's no mistaking it on this occasion, as the finger leaves a smudge in the coagulating crimson coating the concrete floor.

Jada's instincts bellow *get out!* Her legs refuse to comply.

The man's once tanned Greek skin is pale due to blood loss, so how is he moving? Surely they're not really, actually, zombies?

The repairman's arm bends at the elbow. As if doing press-ups, he pushes himself upwards; then his hand slips in his own arterial juices. He face-plants the floor; teeth crack; he doesn't complain. She is almost compelled to offer help, but, deep down, she knows she'll regret it.

Once more the man struggles to all fours, and that's when Jada runs.

The closest car with a price tag is a Mondeo, so she casts aside every key apart from the one with the Ford fob. She has to press the unlock button thrice before the saloon's lights flash. She opens the door, dives in and switches on the ignition. Releasing the handbrake, she hears another wail. It's a kid. As the scream tails off, Jada glances up at the rear view mirror. At the garage's office. Its custodian crosses the threshold, arms aloft, staggering on an ankle that looks broken. He's heading straight for the woman stealing his assets.

Lip curled in disgust, she slams the gear stick into reverse, spins the steering wheel and stomps on the accelerator. Engine whining, tyres screeching, the car flies out of its parking space. Jada aims to ram the mechanic but swerves to miss him at the last minute. She switches to first and roars out of the lot, leaving the zombie in her wake.

Right onto McLeod, then left onto Nelson Drive. Her destination the bypass that'll take her towards the closest motorway. She has to stop suddenly to avoid ploughing into an overturned ambulance, and during the sudden silence, the child, wherever they are, shrieks again.

Wait. I can't just leave a kid to be found by freaks like the one at Mortborough MOT's.

Or should she put herself first? The child will probably die before Jada finds them.

A flash across the rear-view mirror has her spinning in her seat: a little boy, no older than six, sprints across the road.

Brake pedal down.

A skinny, shambling woman chases the boy.

Into reverse.

Woman catches boy. Brings him down.

"No!" Jada guns the engine and backs up, but she's too late. Zombie lady has torn out the child's throat. Dumbly, she gapes at the speeding vehicle, her teeth and chin slick with blood.

"You bitch!" Jada shouts as she brakes.

The rear end of the stopping Mondeo shunts the monster away from her victim, propelling her into a parked van.

Out gets Jada. She runs to the boy, drops to his side, but she's too late. His eyes are glassy, the gash on his pale neck wide and gruesome. Pink bubbles on his lips.

"No, no, no, stay with me, mate, stay with me!" Jada hugs his warm body close. Her hearing his muffled, her vision blurred by tears.

After a few moments, a smash of glass nearby shakes her from her torpor. She looks at the little fellow's angelic face, then at the blood staining her magnolia vest.

I'm staying in town. Not leaving another single child to be eaten alive. I'll prove Evolve are responsible for this shit.

She puts her foot down. Before long, she's in Shawbrook, a high population density area. Known for its issues with anti-social behaviour, the district now has problems of a more dramatic nature. Some zombies wander the streets, while others are too busy gorging themselves on the flesh of those too slow or infirm to escape.

She crests a rise in the road. Suddenly, the way ahead is obstructed by vehicles.

Fuck. Which dickhead's done this?

It's a deliberate roadblock – the cars and vans are carefully parked rather than crashed or abandoned – and it means Jada will have to take a significant detour. She left-turns the Mondeo onto a side street.

Wait a minute. I can drive over the pedestrianised section, can't I? Through that shitty little precinct. Not like I'm gonna get in trouble.

A sharp right, and the saloon's wheels are rumbling on paving flags rather than tarmac. She has to keep left to avoid the row of leafless trees along the terrace. The stretch

77

of shops is no more than fifty yards long, but it will save her at least a mile of driving. More importantly, it's unlikely to be barricaded. And if she comes across any of those nasty —

One minute the way's clear; the next it's not as two men appear from nowhere. Somehow, Jada immediately knows they're not infected. She brakes and swerves, but not quickly enough. The Ford's front bumper clips the taller of the pair.

He spins away. Hits the ground.

The shorter man, head in hands, stares for a moment. First at his friend, then at Jada.

Shit.

Chapter 10 — Lena Adderley — 2.25pm

Other than banks, post offices are probably the most secure of civilian locations. The postmaster of the branch Lena fled into after escaping the lunatics on the B8102 didn't have the foresight to lock himself in the rear of the building. Unlucky for him, but not for her.

The man is lying on the shop floor, his dead hands still holding his excavated intestines.

Slumped in the computer chair, Lena checks her sat-phone again. There's no message, though she does notice a few flakes of blood on her blouse sleeve. Stealing the keys from the manager was a grisly business, but it saved her life, because on six occasions over the last three hours, gangs of maniacs have assaulted the post office. The fourth lot breached the front entrance only to be stopped by the heavier internal door. Eventually, they gave up attempting to gain entry, as did the next two groups to try the same. Perhaps easier pickings passed by outside.

They won't be deterred indefinitely, however.

Although Lena hasn't moved much, she hasn't been idle. She's been in contact with Villeneuve, coordinating quarantine measures. He admitted during their last conversation that military intervention was likely, if not inevitable. Therefore, her time is limited. She has only a few hours to reach company headquarters, find Doctor Sofia Aslam and devise a means of rectifying the situation, one that saves innocent lives but also prevents Evolve from losing the government contract.

You're a fool, Lena. There's no stopping this shit-storm. Losing a contract will be the least of your worries when those animals finally get hold of you. 'Cause they will, in the end. You can't hide in here forever...

No, she can't continue to cower away in here, nor does she plan to. She *shall* locate Dr Aslam; she shall do her best to stop the slaughter. Safeguarding Evolve's reputation and the family name may or may not be a lost cause, but she's not going to surrender. She won't allow the likes of Villeneuve to bully her, either. Adderleys don't bow down to anyone.

With a new-found resolve she stands. She finishes the cola drink she took from the shop fridge, forces herself to eat the second finger of a chocolate bar and takes a puff on her inhaler. The medicine seems to be working. She's been in the open air, but she's not transformed into a demented man-eater. Of course, if she gets bitten, she's still at risk. The chemical – produced by her company, signed off by her own hand, much to Dr Aslam's consternation – would circumvent her respiratory system and the protection offered by the medication. It would be in her bloodstream. Her vegetarianism would be renounced in the strongest of terms.

The medicine is working, so perhaps that means Resurrex can be tweaked after all… Aslam will know.

She shakes the speculation from her mind. Once she's found the scientist, she'll reassess. Her first priority, contrary to her promise to Villeneuve, will be to stop the outbreak. To save lives. Anything else, including saving the aforementioned politician's scaly skin, will be a bonus.

Ridiculously, before leaving, Lena almost checks her pocket mirror. There are narcotically-enraged psychopaths roaming the streets, and she's acting like she's meeting a corporate client. She's in denial, she suspects, still struggling to comprehend the enormity of the day's developments.

Zombies. The fucking undead.

"No," Villeneuve's voice echoes in her mind, "the official line is they're terrorists."

Yeah, right.

The back of the post office is still to be targetted by the 'terrorists', so she'll use that way out. Its substantial steel door opens into a yard, which, save for a couple of half-full parcel cages, is empty. It's open to the elements; a couple of puddles glint in the sunlight. The clouds are clearing a little, the air freshening, but the temperature remains over twenty-five degrees. Lena's nostrils wrinkle at the smell of burning plastic.

None of the keys in her hand work in the pedestrian door, so she depresses a button to open the vehicular egress gates. She grimaces as an ancient motor grinds into life. It's too loud, especially with the metal shutters creaking, groaning and clattering as they raise. As soon as the opening is sufficiently wide, she presses the red stop switch and ducks into the alleyway behind Foster Street.

A glance both ways suggests her exit is undetected. Foster Street leads onto Tintagel Road, which will eventually pass the Civic Hall. She won't follow the route through the shopping district, though. Instead, she'll stick to the backstreets and sidestreets, the ones she recalls from her teenage days.

She was an awkward teenager – tall, gangly, studious – but she was also a keen athlete. Many of her dawns were spent pounding the pavements of Mortborough, and she's kept fit ever since. Hopefully, her stamina and her memory of the town's geography will keep her alive today.

So she runs. As endorphins are released, her fear begins to subside. She trembles when she hears screams, smashing glass or the rumble of charging feet or sudden explosions, but at least she has a plan now. Providing she keeps her wits about her and carries on moving, she'll be alright. Wearing flat shoes, she feels light and nimble. She barely notices the tell-tale signs of chaos she passes; the smoking vehicles, terraced houses with battered front doors and smears of blood on tarmac become a blur.

She even begins to feel more optimistic for the future long term. People have died, and for that she feels remorse, but Evolve's intentions were good. They wanted to help Mother Nature. Do their bit for the ailing environment. Naturally, the prospect of turning a profit while doing so pleased investors, but financial success was never Lena's driving force. In her heart, she still hopes the Mortborough disaster can be remedied.

Priority one – stop the killings.

Priority two – redeem the Adderley reputation.

Priority three – fix Resurrex, save the world.

Of course, if the Army gets involved, these dreams will be quashed. The outbreak will become common knowledge. She and her fellow directors will be charged with corporate manslaughter. Her father's legacy obliterated. The company dead. Their altruistic vision for naught.

Stay positive. Focus on what you can *do, not what might happen. Villeneuve's an arrogant prick, but self-serving, too. He'll hold off for as long as possible, because discretion will benefit him more. Stay positive —*

She freezes: there's a man up ahead. He's just appeared from a street at a right angle to Lena's and is fewer than twenty yards away. Meandering and stumbling, he's either intoxicated, disabled or one of *them*. But he won't see her if he doesn't look to his right. To improve her chances, she hides behind a withered tree at the roadside and waits. Sweat trickles down her spine, between her breasts, down her nose.

Turn around, Lena! Turn and run!

Yet she ignores the urge. She's compelled to peek out and see if he's passed her by but remains motionless. After counting to thirty, she hazards a quick glimpse. The figure has vanished, so on Lena goes, half-sneaking, half-cantering.

Upon reaching the next junction, she approaches with care. She takes a swift look to the right and espies the man, who now appears to be walking faster. Biting her top lip, she bursts forwards and reaches the next street.

She recommences running, but the zombie sighting has spooked her. At any moment she could cross paths with one of *them*, and next time she might be spotted. She's been running for a while and won't have enough energy left to survive a chase.

Now every sound, every scuffle or bang she hears in the bungalows and townhouses she passes, fills her with dread. She needs to be quicker, travel smarter, be safer. Stealing an abandoned car isn't the answer. They're too loud; plus there's the danger she could trigger an alarm and send out an open invitation to any enemies in the vicinity.

The next turn buoys Lena's spirits. Leaning against a street sign, there's a bicycle. It's a BMX, an adolescent's toy, but it'll double her pace without drawing attention. She gives it a cursory inspection and climbs aboard, praying its wheels and pedals aren't squeaky…

They are as quiet as she could hope. Even when she reaches Armitage Road, a flatter, smoother thoroughfare where she begins to build up speed, the bike makes little noise.

Riding hard, she passes bemused locals every fifty yards or so. Each time, they blunder in her direction, hands grasping. But she's too quick, and they're not perceptive enough to anticipate her and block her path. After following her for a few seconds, they return to banging at windows, clumsily walking or doing things to dead bodies that Lena tries not to see.

One thing she can't ignore is that many of the freaks she encounters, when not occupied by food or potential food, are going one way. Slowly but surely, they're heading in the same direction as she is. In fact, the closer she gets to Highgrove Industrial Estate, the greater their number.

She reaches a bend in the road. If she continues, she'll be on the highway which leads into the industrial park. Once she's halfway around the curve, she can see the traffic lights at the junction, where Armitage meets Grainger Road. And that's where she grips the brakes.

Damn. I don't need this right now. Not when I'm so close.

Grainger is swamped. Emerging from the shadow of the old Catholic church on the corner, hundreds of townsfolk are making for Highgrove. They remind her of childhood Saturday afternoons with her dad, and the multitudes heading to Old Trafford for the football. If she takes the same route as them, she'll be in amongst the horde. No matter how fast she pedals, she won't be able to dodge so many.

Now she's incongruous, though. A beacon for the monsters behind her as well as some of those crossing the road fifty yards in front.

Suddenly, it dawns on her: she has hostiles on all sides. Individuals break away from the main crowd. Not many, but enough. They scramble towards her, dodging crashed cars and bollards. Swallowing, Lena turns in her saddle. Numerous wild-looking walkers are becoming runners. In all, roughly thirty zombies are converging on her position. More are on the way with every passing second.

I'm fucked. Really, well and truly fucked.

All roads lead to Evolve plc. Lena, almost at the disaster's epicentre, ignored Dr Aslam's warnings about Resurrex, and she will pay the ultimate price for her recklessness. Unless…

Is that church door open? Or is it a trick of the light?

She drops the cycle and sprints towards salvation.

Chapter 11 — Jada Blakowska — 3pm

He's moving.

"He's moving, your friend, he's moving!"

"Great." The diminutive man doesn't move a muscle. He certainly doesn't smile.

"He's stopped now."

In fact, since they arrived in the butcher's shop, Brad hasn't said a word. Although seeing his friend getting run over must've been a shock, it shouldn't have caused this level of despair. But, Jada supposes, he may have seen worse over the last few hours. It's been a hell of a day.

Luke's eyelids flutter, and he coughs.

"Hey," Jada says, "stay with us."

Suddenly, the ruggedly-handsome man sits bolt upright. His arms shoot out, as if he's warding off a blow. Eyes wide, he glares at the strange woman.

"Woah." Jada kneels by the prostrate man's side. "You've had quite a knock, so you need to take it easy." She glances at Brad for support, but he doesn't make eye contact. Instead, he continues to tap the wooden counter he's sat at with the cleaver he's found.

"Who are you?" Luke blinks. He's staring at Jada like she's some sort of exotic snake.

"My name's Jada. I'm a reporter. I… ran you over, about half an hour ago. I'm sorry. Your friend and I carried you in here, and… well, that's about it."

"Where's Connor?"

"I… what? Who's Connor, sorry?"

"My boy… he's… Brad, help me out 'ere…"

"Ain't found 'im yet, bro," Brad replies dully.

"What 'bout LaRosa? Briony?"

The smaller man shakes his head. He begins to speak, but his voice cracks, and he sobs instead.

"Shit… I remember… sorry, mate, I… fuck, can't believe I just said that…"

A whistle and thud makes Jada jump; Brad has chopped the counter with the butcher's knife. Jada gives him a tight smile; he doesn't react.

"You've got concussion, I think." Jada touches the injured fellow's shoulder. "I hit you pretty hard."

Luke scowls. "Why'd ya hit me?"

"I didn't 'hit you' hit you. I was driving, and you ran in front of my car."

"You were driving on a pedestrianised area, though, weren't ya? It'll be on CCTV. So I could sue you."

"Yes, I was. Yes, you could. I don't know if you've noticed, though, but we're in the middle of a zombie attack. I was doing what I had to, to survive. "

"Shit, yeah. Sorry. I need t' find Connor."

Images of a small boy being chased then savaged by a female zombie flash across Jada's mind's eye. She gulps. "How old is he?"

"Connor? Eleven. Why?"

"I saw a kid dying —"

"— Where? When?" Luke stands, agitated, and sways a little. He steadies himself against the display refrigerator.

"It's okay. This kid was young, five year old, or something. Just try and relax. Do you hurt anywhere?"

"No. Well, yeah. Nothing major. My ribs are achin' a bit. And my leg. But we need to go. Brad?"

The other man turns to his friend slowly.

"We good?"

"Yeah."

Jada frowns. "You still seem a little woozy. Sure you're okay to be out there?" She looks at the barricaded door, at the empty parade outside.

"I'm fine." Luke does look more lucid as he steals cooked meats from the deli counter. "We'll just grab somethin' to eat, 'n' we'll dust."

"Right. Do you have any idea what's going on here?"

"Not a clue. People —"

"— Zombies, they're zombies." Brad interrupts.

"Whatever. Anyway, they're just goin' mental 'n' killing each other." As they clear debris from the front door, he tells of the outbreak at his workplace, then the ill-fated trip to save LaRosa.

"Shit." Jada keeps an eye on Brad: his movements are mechanical, his expression inscrutable. "Then you came straight here?"

"No, well yeah, we were goin' this way, towards Connor's house, but a massive group of those things got in the way. We 'ad t' find somewhere t' hide."

Brad removes the final chair from the entrance and stands back.

"This butcher's was the only shop without smashed doors. So we holed up 'ere, just till we knew they were gone, 'n' we were on our way back out when you showed up." When Brad makes to open the door, Luke stops him. "Woah, slow down, buddy. Let's see 'ow the land lies first, eh?" He looks out of the shop, left, then right. "All clear, for now." He grabs a knife, as do Jada and Brad, and he opens the door. "What 'bout you?"

Following him across the precinct, Jada tells her story. They've reached the roadblock that stopped her earlier by the time she's finished. "You sure we shouldn't just use the car?"

"Very sure." Luke wipes perspiration from his brow as he peers through one of the blockade cars windows. The temperature is high, though new dark clouds are blowing this way. "They've got good ears, these things. Besides, Mortborough's a small town, innit?"

"Yeah, but when you're in a car, you're protected, aren't you? Even if they do hear you, they can't get at you, can they?"

"No. Unless you crash, or run into a block-up like this. Then they know exactly where you are."

"I guess."

"That's when you die," Brad says, matter-of-fact.

"C'mon. We'll take the next left." Luke skirts the roadblock and runs at a half-crouch to a house with tall, leaf-free hedges. He stops behind one of the hedgerows to catch his breath. "So," he whispers when Jada catches up, "you gonna report on all this, or somethin'?"

"I'll try." Jada peeks out from behind the greenery. They're in a more affluent area now; the houses are grander, mostly detached, with gardens instead of yards. The next street is empty.

"Don't ya reckon we've got enough on our plate without you doin' yer intrepid journalist act?"

'We've,' he said. Are we a team now?

"It won't slow us down. I lost my camera when I first saw the zombies. I've taken a couple of photos with my phone, but the battery's low, so I'm keeping it switched off till there's mobile signal. I'll just be takin' notes when I get chance. The next street is clear."

"Weird, innit, how nobody's phone's workin'?"

"Yeah. Bit more than weird, if you ask me."

The trio turn the corner, staying low. They sprint to the first parked vehicle they see, a hatchback, and hunker down behind it.

"Have you killed any?" asks Jada.

"Yeah." Luke gives his friend the briefest of glances. Then he looks through the car's windows to scope out the road ahead. "But we won't talk 'bout that. D' ya reckon ya killed the one ya rammed?"

"I think so." She recalls the child killer's broken body, lay close to the boy she'd just caught. "I was braking when I hit her, but she slammed into another car pretty hard."

"*It.*" Brad is looking in the opposite direction to ensure they're not being pursued. "They ain't 'he' or 'she' now. Just 'it'." His gaze narrows. "Think we got a tail."

"Yeah?" Luke stares at the last turn off they took. "Can't see shit."

"The hedge we just hid behind." Her back to the car, Jada points. "It's rustlin'. Shakin' about."

"Just the wind," Luke surmised. "C'mon, let's —"

"— There *is* no wind now." Brad scurries around the Vauxhall Astra to take cover.

"Good point." Luke follows.

Joining them, Jada draws the wickedly sharp knife she took from the rack at the butcher's. "I'll carry on watching this way," she says, "and you two scout on ahead. If we can reach the next turn before it sees us, we can shake it off."

"Good idea." Luke scampers away, with Brad close behind.

Using the palm of her hand, Jada rubs grit from sore eyes. The privet is still wobbling, as if an animal is trapped inside. She looks over her shoulder. Luke and Brad have reached the corner of the next road. A thumbs up from the former indicates the way is clear. Then he gesticulates. He and his friend hide behind a telephone exchange terminal.

Jada realises why: a bloody hand and half an arm are protruding from the bush. Then the upper arm, the shoulder, a man's face. Black, dry blood on his lips and jowls. Fresh red where the hedge's thorns have scratched his pallid skin. With a final flourish, he escapes the brambles, tearing off half of his football jersey in the process.

She looks back to her new companions.

Luke's peering from behind the green metal box. "Get down!" he mimes.

Cursing herself, Jada obeys. *It must've seen me. I was gawpin' at it for at least five seconds.*

Uneven steps are getting closer.

Shit, shit, shit. "Help me, guys," she mouths at Luke.

He shrugs, not as if he doesn't care, but because he doesn't know what to do. He turns. To confer with Brad, presumably.

Still the zombie's coming; Jada can now hear wet noises, as if a pig is snuffling for truffles.

Wait a minute. There's three of us, one of it. It's the asshole, not us. We're just trying to get on with life. Finding courage from somewhere, Jada springs to her feet.

The creature responds instantly. Its stride lengthens. It waddles as it hurries her way, jaws working, saliva and blood drooling, fingers flexing. Eyes bloodshot and unblinking.

The newswoman hears a commotion behind her. No doubt Luke and Brad are panicking about her sudden act of defiance. As the fiend gets closer, Jada wonders if she's gone mad. It looks oafish but strong, over six feet in height, muscles showing through the rips in its shirt. Perhaps she picked the wrong battle. She holds her knife high. The stainless steel catches sunlight as it quivers.

And suddenly, she's not alone. Brad's to her left, Luke to her right. All are holding blades, all ready to fight back and slay the beast before them.

It doesn't stand a chance. The three humans strike simultaneously: Jada spears its right eye; Luke stabs horizontally under its outstretched left arm, plunging deep into its side; Brad all but severs its right arm at the shoulder with his heavy cleaver. For a moment, the zombie is pinned in place. Blood pumps and sprays, but its expression remains one of casual malice.

Abruptly it sags, wrenching the three daggers from their wielders. Jada, Luke and Brad look at each other, at the zombie's blood on their clothes and skin. The former laughs, and bizarrely, so do his comrades. They retrieve their weapons and leave the dead man in the road.

"Shit," says Jada. "That was intense."

"Are you fuckin' mental, or somethin'?" Luke's still smiling. "Why didn't ya just run?"

"I dunno. Just… I just thought 'fuck it'."

Brad's grin has faded, but there's a new resolve in his features. "C'mon, let's bounce. Warrencroft's not far."

"Yeah, so?" Luke hurries to keep up. "We're goin' for Connor, right? The Warren isn't on the way."

"No. But, it ain't much of a detour, 'n' it'll be safer walkin' through the park than it will on the streets."

"He's right," says Jada. "Fewer people about, fewer zombies, less looking over our shoulder. Could be quicker as a result."

"Fair dues," says Luke. "But from now on, we stick together. No splittin' up, no scoutin' ahead, no leavin' people behind t' cover us. Sorry about that, Jada. We shouldn't have left ya behind that car."

"No worries. It was my idea."

A couple of alleyways later, they're on the edge of Warrencroft Country Park. When they see one of the playgrounds, Jada feels a prickle of nostalgia. She and her schoolmates rollerbladed here. Or they did until drink, drugs and boys become more alluring. As an only child, her friends were her life, till they began to drift away to other cities and countries, or found husbands, had kids. None were as career-focussed as Jada.

She wants to ask Luke about his son. She knows enquiring could trigger Brad's depression, though. He must've lost someone close today, but he's been tight-lipped thus far. Even so, Jada needs to know more about the child she's risking her life trying to find. It's ludicrous, really: she's known Luke and Brad for just a few hours, yet she acquiesced with their suicide rescue mission without a second thought. Does that make her a hero, or just an idiot?

"'Ere we are," says Brad, pointing at a gate in the park fence. "First left towards the maze, round that, then straight on."

Although Luke believes there's a quicker route, he doesn't press the point.

Through they go, then left.

By the time they react to the sound in the closest bushes, they are too late. It's not the undead that menace them, however. A man and a woman, dressed as if for battle, have the three of them at gunpoint before they can even think about running. He's huge and skinheaded like a nightclub bouncer, while she looks like she's just stepped out of a beauty salon.

"Don't move," the male says, his accent Scottish.

Chapter 12 — Harry Lunt — 16:00

"Orders are orders," the woman intones. "Chain of command, an' all that."

Bullshit. This is fucked.

"Aye, so ye keep sayin'."

"So what are we waitin' for?"

"Jesus, am ah speakin' in Swahili, or somethin'? For the third time, I want tae speak tae Ms Adderley before we start executin' civilians."

Anderson stretches out on the drawing room chaise longue. The miniature castle is luxurious within, which is probably why the owners charge a fortune for weddings. "Adderley's not in charge, as you well know, Lunt. This is a government op —"

"— 'N' she's a consultant. She has a right tae be consulted."

"Villeneuve said confidentiality trumps everything else. The woman, that Jada, I'm pretty sure she was under surveillance recently. One of the grunts at HQ was talking about a good looking, half-black, half-Polish freelancer based in Manchester, poking her nose into Adderley —"

"— Ye don't know that's her, fer fucksake!"

"Maybe, maybe not. But she admitted she's a reporter. She'll talk. She'll share her story on Twitter an' Instagram an' wherever else. Which means we won't get paid. Or worse."

Lunt breathes deeply through his nose for a moment. "But we took her phone, and wiped the photos, so she'll struggle tae share 'em anywhere, won't she?"

"So? Her phone will've already backed them up, to the cloud."

"There's no data connection, though, is there? You switched off the mobile towers, remember?"

"Maybe. But orders are orders. Chain of command to respect —"

"— If yer just gonnae keep repeatin' yerself, Anderson, can ye do it someplace else? I've got a sore head."

And how. That cunt Luke had some punch on him.

"Fair enough." Anderson affects an air of indifference. "Just never thought I'd see the day Harry Lunt went soft."

"What ye talking about?"

"You wanna speak to Lena, I get that. But I don't think that's the main reason you're lettin' those three live."

"Oh aye?" Lunt stands and almost bangs his head on the bear's head mounted on the wall above his chair. "Educate me, then. Why am I lettin' 'em live?"

"Ya never liked hurtin' civvies. Even abroad. But you always used to grit yer teeth 'n' do it anyway. Now something's changed."

"Bullshit."

"Okay. Have it your way. But when we finally do get hold of Lena, she'll either tell us that crowd control's not her remit, or she'll say 'yes, kill the locals', to save her precious company's reputation. But we won't get hold of her in here, will we? We won't be able to find her if we're babysittin' these village idiots."

"Actually, that's not strictly true. I have a plan —"

"— It's almost as if you don't want to speak to her. You don't want to be told it's okay to kill civvies."

"Have you heard yerself? You're soundin' paranoid. This job is gettin' to ye. 'N' anyway, genius, what happens when HQ tells us Lena is outta the loop? What excuse would I have then?"

Anderson takes a swig of the water she stole from the castle/house's gift shop. She grins broadly. "HQ can't tell us shit. You 'lost' yer sat-phone, remember." She mimes speech marks when she says "lost".

"Aye, but ah didnae know yours wouldnae work, did ah?" Lunt is losing his temper. Not due to his integrity being questioned, but because his associate is right: he doesn't want to kill anyone without good reason. These three kids they found don't deserve death; they're simply in the wrong place at the wrong time.

"I'll give ya that. Maybe this isn't all planned out. But either way, Lunt, I need to know if yer losing yer stomach for dirty work."

"Why? Why do you 'need to know'? What'll you do?"

She doesn't answer. Instead, she raises her hand for silence.

"What?"

"Just listen."

Someone, or *something*, is moving nearby. Within the walls of the castle.

Both agents retrieve their weapons and move towards the drawing room's outsized door. Anderson, leading, moves into the corridor fluidly, her MP5 pointing at the elaborately-detailed ceiling. "Clear," she hisses.

"Alarm's no' been triggered," Lunt whispers. "Don't reckon we've been breached."

"The prisoners, then?"

"Aye, prob'ly. While we've been arguin' about 'em, they've been takin' advantage."

"I secured them —"

"— Obviously not well enough."

"Shit. Shit shit shit."

Down the passageway they go, watched by the forbidding eyes of Warrencroft's watercolour-immortalised aristocracy. It's gloomy in here, even with the chandeliers lit. Probably haunted, too. According to Lena, who took Lunt on a guided tour years ago, a headless man roams these curio-cluttered hallways every night.

The three civilians are being detained in the windowless kitchen, the door of which is still locked. Lunt turns the ornate key in its lock; the movements on the other side cease.

"I'm goin' in." Anderson readies her submachine gun. Her jaw set, she intends to atone for her sloppiness.

Lunt nods. *The eagerness of youth? Or is the younger agent startin' tae lose her composure amidst the carnage 'n' panic?* "Right behind ye."

She bursts into the kitchen. "Freeze!"

Dreading overzealous gunfire, her comrade is hot on her heels.

The two men, Luke and Brad, are sitting on the floor, their backs to twin ovens. Jada, the woman, sits on a counter, next to the pot-wash unit. All three look at their captors with blank expressions. "Is there a problem?" the latter asks, the confusion on her face giving way to hostility.

"What've yous been doin' in here?" Anderson demands.

"Doin'?" Luke, whose eye is swelling where Lunt backhanded him earlier, holds his hands out for inspection. They're still fastened together by cable ties. "What do ya think we've been *doin'*? Sat 'ere, waiting for you two psychos to let us go."

"False imprisonment, this," Brad snipes belligerently as he struggles to his feet without the assistance of his hands. "Just 'cause there's zombies out there, don't mean ya can lock us up."

"Aye. Ye said that already," Lunt replies, but not unkindly. *These kids have probably suffered enough for one day, 'n' now we're treatin' 'em like animals.*

"It'd be a lot worse if I had my way," Anderson warns, before shooting a look the Scotsman's way. "Believe me. Now, I wanna see your wrists too, both o' yous."

Brad complies immediately, thrusting his bound wrists in her face.

"Woah," Anderson snaps, her face becoming flushed. "Back the fuck away, shithead." She shoves him hard, and he lands on his rear.

She needs tae calm down. This fucked-up town 'n' its fucked-up locals have spooked her.

Jada steps over Brad. "Here," she says. But when she reaches out to present her arms, she does so quickly, whilst lunging forwards. She's slipped her manacles. Must be double-jointed. As Jada grabs Anderson's SMG, she pushes it in Lunt's direction. Shots ring out, deafening in the confined space. One misses Lunt by a hair's breadth. In a split-second he has to decide whether to level his own gun or concentrate on stopping Jada's frenzied attack.

He chooses the second option.

Straightaway, he is foiled; Luke barrels into him. The younger man uses his cable-conjoined hands to first hammer Lunt's gun from his hands, then strike at his face.

The male agent recovers to block, sweeps Luke's legs and turns his attention to Anderson and Jada. They're still grappling over the MP5. He's about to grab the crazed prisoner when Brad, who's almost upright, dives headlong at the three brawlers. Short but compact, he knocks Lunt off-balance.

As a result, Lunt's right hand, which was reaching for Jada's arm, slams onto the top of Anderson's shoulder instead. Suddenly, her SMG swings downwards. It fires again. Only once this time, but blood spurts.

Anderson grunts in pain. She sinks to her knees, and the MP5 slips from her fingers.

Immediately, Jada reels away. "Oh, god." She raises a red-speckled hand to her mouth.

Lunt scoops his shotgun up and fires once; the three locals flinch at the noise. "Stop now. All of ye. Get on the ground. Quick-smart."

Luke and Brad are already down, and now Jada joins them. Lunt takes three cable ties and secures the prisoners, then squats beside Anderson. She's hit bad. Femoral artery, maybe, which will mean death in seconds if the blood loss can't be stemmed. He grabs a pair of oven mitts and wraps them around her thigh. When he pulls them tight, Anderson lets out a cry. "Keep pressure on it," he urges her, but she's barely conscious.

As the claret flow slows to a trickle, the former soldier blows a long breath. "Fuck. Ah fuckin' knew…" *she needed tae chill out.* He finishes the thought silently, for he doesn't want his captives to realise how shaken he is.

Ah need tae get a grip. I've seen worse than this. Or have I? This is different: the enemy don't fire back, like they did in Sarajevo, Sierra Leone, Helmand et cetera, but they bite. They fuckin' eat each other! It's… different, more disturbing. No wonder Anderson lost her shit.

"What ya gonna do with us?" Luke says.

"Yeah, bro," Brad chimes in, "you can't just keep us 'ere."

"I got a kid I need t' save," Luke adds.

Leaning with both hands on a chest freezer, Lunt keeps his eyes closed.

Jada clears her throat. "There are all sorts of kids and adults that need savin'. Listen, I know you probably have your orders. And you probably think those orders are the most important thing right now, 'cause if you just forget your orders, you're kinda surrendering to the chaos of all this…"

They're fuckin' eating other! Seen some shite in m' time, seen genocide, torture, but this…

"… To stick together, not fight each other. Right? 'Cause if we don't…"

Now Anderson's on her way out, 'n' Lena was prob'ly caught hours ago, while I'm sittin' in here, listenin' tae these daft English cunts…

"'Ey, mate," Luke says. "Are you still with us, or what?"

Suddenly Lunt's sensory feedback clarifies, as if a switch has been flicked. Over the years, he's learned to trust his instincts when they come to the fore. He turns away from the wall, cocks his head to one side. "Shh."

Simultaneously, the three Mortboronians ask questions.

Lunt merely raises a clenched fist and hushes his audience once more. "Outside. *Them.* Mustae heard the gunfire."

"Thank your friend for that," Jada mutters.

Lunt leaves the kitchen, walks down the hallway, into the lobby. He peers through the stained glass in the barred windows by the front door. Some of the shadows are tinted red, some blue, some yellow. All are headed this way.

Shit. At least thirty o' the fuckers from this direction alone. Could easily be quadruple that in all. 'N' I'm stuck in here, in a buildin' right in the middle of a fuckin' field. My only backup three fuckin' civvies.

Jesus wept.

Chapter 13 — Luke Norman — 16:35

Bang, bang, bang on the doors.

They have four guns – a modern-looking shotgun, a small machine gun, two pistols. Enough for one apiece, and sufficient bullets to shoot every one of the one hundred or so zombies four times each. In his teens, Brad was in a gang, so he's handled firearms. Luke's fired shotguns and .22s on his dad's farm on the other side of Manchester. Jada spent a short stint in the Territorial Army as a twenty year-old. And Lunt would probably marry an assault rifle if the law permitted. The odds of four people with such knowledge of weaponry being together in a small English suburb are astronomical. It's the sort of plot armour bestowed by any B-movie one might care to name.

Except that this particular tale has a twist. The resident hardboiled army veteran, who is something of a cliché himself, is a control freak. "No," he reiterates, pacing the kitchen. "I'm no' dolin' out service weapons tae civvies. Ah don't care how much PlayStation ye've played —"

Bang, bang, bang, on the front door and the back.

"Why d' ya keep sayin' that?" Brad interrupts. "We've. All. Fired. Actual. Weapons."

"Aye, so ye say." Using duct tape found in a caretaker's tool box, he secures two MP5 magazines together. He repeats the trick with another pair, then a third.

"Listen, Lunt," Jada says, rubbing at her wrists where the cable ties bit into her flesh. "We're not gonna try to escape. We just want to defend ourselves. We have a *right* to defend ourselves."

"Not wi' *my* equipment, ye don't."

"That's where yer wrong." Luke is whetting the knife he stole from the butcher's, as his dad taught him when they used to dress their kills. It takes his mind off the aches incurred when Jada ran him over and when Lunt and Anderson subdued him. Plus it distracts him from the gut-contorting fear that his son's been slaughtered.

"Oh aye?"

"Aye. 'Cause if it wasn't fer you locking us up 'ere, in a house accessible from all four sides, we might be somewhere safer."

"Where's safer than a fuckin' castle?"

Brad is looking through the tool box, comparing hammers. "Anywhere that 'asn't 'ad a proper loud machine gun fired in it recently."

Lunt's face loses some its stoniness.

We're right, 'n' that Jock bastard knows it. "You 'n' yer trigger-happy pal got us in this shit." Luke's arms are folded. "If she hadn't lost 'er cool 'n' opened fire, we'd be safe. Least ya can do is let us fight our way through it."

The former army officer shakes his head, but more in resignation than disagreement

Bang, bang, bang – this time from three of the castle's walls, not two.

"There's no way you can defend us against attacks from all four directions," Jada points out. "Ex-army, ex-special forces or not. You can't take on over a hundred of those monsters on your own."

"Right, okay." Lunt slams a meaty right fist on the bain marie, rattling metal covers and spoons. "But," he raises the forefinger of his left hand, "as soon as those fuckers are dead or gone, ye give me the guns back. Alright? I need yer word on that. Nae tricks like Jada pulled before."

The three civilians share a glance.

"Yer word, now, or the cable ties are goin' back on."

Luke, Jada and Brad nod their assent.

"Right. I keep the SPAS." He hefts his shotgun. "You were TA, right?"

Jada nods. "Army Reserve, they call it now."

"Aye, they do. Used an SA80?"

She nods again.

She's a cool customer, that one, but feisty when she needs t' be. Good looking, too…

"You take the MP, then." He hands her the submachine gun. "You two, take these." Lunt gives Luke and Brad his and Anderson's sidearms with a wry grin. "Ah must be fuckin' tapped. Try not tae shoot yerselves, okay?"

Despite himself, Luke feels a thrill as he grips the surprisingly-light Sig Sauer P226. He's shot at rabbits, pigeons and even a deer once. Now he'll have human beings in his sights. Undead ones, of course, but flesh-and-blood humans all the same. He blinks a few times, almost overwhelmed by his new-found power and responsibility.

To his father's chagrin, Luke never enjoyed murdering defenceless animals; he wonders how he'll fare when he's filling people with lead. His dad would be fine, he suspects. *I wonder if the old man'll get caught up in all this, over in Atherbury.* Christopher Norman, a widower, lives with his daughter Maddie and his youngest son Mason in a remote spot in the shadow of the Pennines. It would be a safe place to take Connor – if the lad can be found.

"They're no' people, remember," Lunt says. His accent is different, of course, but his gravelly tones remind Luke of his father. "They're somethin' else now. Somethin' that'll kill us if we don't kill them." He points at the handgun. "There's the safety switch. 'N' ye reload it like this." The towering Scot gives a brief demonstration, then returns the P226 to Luke. "Squeeze the trigger, don't jerk at it. Aim fer the head, but wait till they're close enough tae be sure."

Bang, bang, and now glass is smashing, this time from the opposite side of the building to the kitchen. All four sides of the fortress, all four of its entrances, are under siege.

Luke feels his senses sharpening: the smell of white wine vinegar used to clean surfaces; the cold, solid steel of the pistol; individual hairs sprouting from Lunt's nostrils. Most pressing, though, is the racket caused by the zombies outside.

"Ah want you on the west side of the building, Luke. There's a wee room, a 'drawing room', wi' a barred window raised off the ground. Stand on the grand piano, 'n' ye'll have a good view o' the entrance on that side."

"What if they break through that entrance?"

"Not gonnae happen. Me 'n' Anderson recce'd this gaffe, 'n' all four doors are virtually bombproof. All the windows are barred 'n' high up off the ground. The zombies'd probably get in eventually, but they won't if yer peppering 'em wi' rounds. We keep firin', we'll be okay."

Lunt turns away to show Brad how to use the Glock.

Suddenly, Luke feels lost, cast adrift. He takes a hit on his inhaler, but he does so more from nervousness than anything else. His e-cig offers scant comfort, too. In a few moments, he'll be up against the horde, alone. Just eight hours ago, he was dreading the start of his shift at work. He would give anything to be back in the office, taking calls from ornery Union Gas customers rather than facing demented undead.

"Go now, son," Lunt says over his shoulder. "West wall. Wee room. Grand piano. Fire through the window. Aim fer the head. Take yer time. Make yer shots count."

"I'm goin'." And Luke's feet are taking him out of the kitchen. He returns Jada's brief smile and wonders if he'll see her again. He'll be sorry if not, because she seems like a good person.

Hot, too — fucksake, Luke, focus!

"Good luck," Brad calls; he's to be posted in the utility room next to the kitchen, which lends a mirror image vantage point to Luke's destination.

"You too."

Down the main corridor he goes, away from the main entrance. Past the only suite on the ground floor, where Anderson is fading away. The first door on the left leads to a ballroom now used for corporate events, the second to a bar. He takes the third, which is signed 'Mr Latham's Chambers'. Already, the din is getting louder.

They can't get in, the captain said. They have plenty of ammunition, so if the defenders keep firing, they'll survive.

But if we keep firin' we keep makin' noise. Which means the zombies keep comin'. 'N' eventually, our guns'll run dry, 'n' we'll be fucked.

He climbs onto the piano. As Lunt promised, he can see the west entrance. Or, he would be able to were it not mobbed by ugly, filthy, blood-daubed fiends. There are at least twenty-five, maybe thirty of them, and they're about fifteen yards away. The window's open in here, so he can smell their sour milk/faeces signature scent.

Luke pushes the window wide and, leaning on the sill, angles his upper body into a firing position. Thus far, the zombies are oblivious to his presence. They're like piranhas sniffing meat. Single-minded, *hive-minded*, intent on gaining entry. He points his weapon at the closest: a short, squat man with a cranium like a medicine ball. He wants an easy shot, something to boost his confidence.

Safety off. Squeeze the trigger. Boom.

Unlike the Glock Brad's using, the Sig Sauer isn't suppressed. Straightaway, Luke realises he's drawn the short straw. Although the zombie in his sights spins away, the exit wound in its head a satisfying mess, the pistol's report summons the attention of at least half a dozen invaders. Most continue to batter the oaken door, but the handful who responded to the gunshot cease their assault. They stare at the human for a moment, like dogs who've sniffed a treat in a stranger's pocket.

Fuck. Do I just keep shootin', or what?

Yes, Lunt said, and he's the expert. Rumbles of MP5, SPAS-12 and Glock fire to the north, east and south indicate everyone else is firing at will. So Luke follows suit. His second effort leaves a zombie shorn of its left ear, bleeding copiously, yet still standing.

He corrects his aim and looses three more rounds, twitching his hands between kills to target the fiends looking his way. All three attempts are successful.

Norman 4, Evil Undead Fuckers 0.

Luke's barrage is prompting a bigger reaction than he expected. More and more of the creatures are forgetting the door to defy the death-dealing man in the window. Snarling, drooling, they leap onto the castle's parapet and scramble towards their tormenter.

"Fuck."

He manages four more shots, three of them splattering brains and blood over their neighbours, before he has to pull his arm back through the bars to safety. He slams the window shut.

Pale, fumbling appendages chase his own. Contorted faces follow, their features mashing against the bars. Teeth splinter; noses crunch; hair sticks to the metal. Hands hammer at the broad pane of glass, breaching it in multiple places at once. Shards tinkle on the drawing room floor and furniture.

Soon, it seems every zombie in Mortborough is straining against the cast iron. The bars begin to creak and shift. Particles of plaster cascade, making a sticky paste with the blood they sprinkle. This isn't a true castle; its defences were installed to repel highwaymen, not armies. With enough numbers, the zombies will break in at some point.

Terror speeds Luke's hands. There are so many targets, so close, that he can't miss. He fires round after round into the press of heads, until the windowsill and bars are slickly crimson. Till he's emptied three and a half clips. Somewhere between a minute and an hour passes.

They stop coming.

Is that it? 'Ave I won?

Luke's breathing slows, and suddenly his arms are like lead. He allows the P226 muzzle to drop and backs away from the ruined, disembodied death-masks and the dark puddle on the carpet. His ears are ringing, the stenches of gore and his own sweat overpowering. Blood is in his mouth. He almost vomits, but he realises it's his own vital fluid; he's bitten his own lip. How many people has he killed?

Abruptly, he has to turn away, needs to avert his eyes.

"Bro?" Brad calls from somewhere else in the building. "You alright, bro?"

In a daze, Luke leaves Mr Latham's Chambers and heads back to the kitchen. He, Brad and Jada stare at each other for a few seconds, their eyes intense yet vacant. They share a wordless embrace as Lunt rejoins them.

Of the foursome, only the ex-squaddie speaks; in fact, he's almost ebullient. "We did it, guys! We only went 'n' fuckin' did it!"

The others eventually smile, but they're hollow expressions, tainted by trauma.

Luke doesn't move for at least five minutes. He's the last to return his borrowed weapon to Lunt. "Right. Now I'm going to find my son."

"Ach." Lunt rubs the back of his own neck. "Sorry, but I cannae let you go."

"You what?" Jada seethes.

"I need to stay wi' Anderson. I cannae leave her."

Jada says, "We might find medical supplies if we leave —"

"— The fuck's that gotta do with us anyway?" Brad demands. "That bitch would've killed us if it wasn't fer you. We're leavin'. With or without you."

Lunt shakes his head. "We'll be easier tae rescue if we're all together —"

"— I don't wanna be rescued," Luke argues. "I wanna find my kid."

"I… I'm sorry." Lunt reloads his Glock and chambers a round. He doesn't aim the gun at anyone, but his demeanour brooks no debate. "Yer all stayin' put, fer now."

Chapter 14 — Lena Adderley — 17:40

The sole heir to the Adderley family fortune has never been religious. She sees survival of the fittest played out on a daily basis in the world of business, and the apocalyptic turn of events in Mortborough is further validation for her atheist beliefs. After all, what kind of deity would permit the horrors visited that day upon her innocent Manchester suburb? She's aware of the free will defence, but there's no rationalising today's events.

However, Lena was given cause to question her lack of faith when she fled into St Paul the Apostle's. The entry wasn't barred by heavenly energy against the zombies in pursuit. Lightning bolts didn't strike them down. The holy water she spilt when she upended the font by the entrance didn't scald their shambling feet like acid. But the godless monsters hankering after her brains and guts seemed to slow down.

It was just your imagination, you idiot. Adrenaline slowing down time, making you faster, or something.

In any case, she made it into the sacristy. Its medieval door, a quarter ton of wood and iron studs, was bolted shut, her persecutors foiled. After a couple of hours of fruitless ramming and knocking, the undead gave up and drifted out of St Paul's, no doubt recommencing their pilgrimage to Evolve.

With the threat gone, Lena was able to make for the same destination. Obviously, she couldn't follow in the zombies' footsteps. But without them battering away at the door, she was able to think. Recalling the urban myths of her childhood, she found a priest's hole, and its adjoining tunnel took her under Grainger Road. The dank, subterranean passageway led to a fifteenth-century coaching inn recently converted into a swanky bar.

When she got to the other end of the subway, she found that provenance had smiled upon her once more. At some point, two of the public house's staff had evidently tried to evade the enemy by going in the opposite direction, towards St Paul's. Perhaps they believed the church would offer divine protection. They didn't make it; they were killed and partially eaten within feet of the passageway's threshold. Their blood and innards glistened in the wan light of the torches they dropped.

Again, timing favoured Lena: the unfortunate bartenders had managed to get the tunnel door open before they succumbed.

Lena left The Wayward Inn via a poorly-barricaded tradesman's exit. Barbed wire topped the wall at the rear of the back yard, so she went back inside and found pliers – plus a hammer, which she tucked into her Prada belt – in a drawer under the pub's bar. She made short work of the wire. Through a thin thicket of nude trees she went, then across rail tracks, and over some railings.

And now she stands in the disused loading bay of a long-closed toy factory. Rain is falling again, refilling puddles that'd almost dried. Lena's at the wrong end of Highgrove Industrial Estate. There are no zombies nearby; the smells of oil and dust are stronger than the rot of dying skin and muscle. She can't leave Tiny Tyke's compound via its main exit, however. That would be the most direct route to Evolve HQ, but it'll take her too close to the horde.

So she'll take the long way around. It's too humid and hot for travelling from unit to unit by scaling fences and snipping barbed wire, but she has no other option if she's to avoid the predators flooding the area.

I have to do this for Dad. I need to keep going no matter what.

Her expensive clothes are snagged and torn. She scratches her hands, her arms and legs, and she leaves hair and blood on barbs, her sweat on meshed metal. By six PM, she's filthy, stinging, aching, yet determined and motivated. Tiny Tyke, Photo-24, Synergy Gas and Barrowclough Aggregates are in her wake.

Stop the killings. Redeem the Adderley reputation. Fix Resurrex. Save the world. No big deal.

She winces as she steps in a pool of dirty water that's deeper than it looks.

Wet socks. No biggie. Just keep going.

Somewhere nearby, a gun discharges, a burst of automatic fire. *Is it Harry and Anderson?*

Skirting forklift trucks and mail cages, Lena crosses DDN's Manchester distribution depot. She's been a large industrial company's director for five years, but these are places she's never seen. Every time Dad said she should visit the shop floor, she declined. Board rooms, spreadsheets, conference calls: they were her domain. Now she's slumming it, amidst the machinery and conveyor belts.

But no workers, of course. They're all dead or worse, thanks to Resurrex, thanks to my firm.

She stops for a moment to catch her breath and use her inhaler. When she leans on a terminal, she nudges a switch, and a motor somewhere whirs into action. "Shit!" She presses a red button immediately; the noise ceases.

Something's heard. There's movement. The roll of a metal canister, perhaps, and... someone walking. Clumsy, uncoordinated, lurching footfalls, undeniably undead.

Heart pounding, Lena ducks behind a cellophane-wrapped crate secured to a pallet. Still the steps fall, neither faster nor slower than they were ten seconds ago. She pulls the claw hammer from her belt, but in doing so, she has to extend her right leg.

Something sees. The footsteps quicken. Getting closer. Hugging the box, she gets ready to run. Now she hears more than the thing's tread. It's wheezing and gurgling, as if its throat's been cut. It stops. No more than six feet away, on the other side of the loaded pallet, the zombie waits. It's quiet now, almost silent, but Lena can still sense its presence.

She cringes. Listens intently. The container behind her creaks and shifts: her hunter is climbing onto it. Suddenly, there's a gasp, and it's there, above her. Drooling as it prepares to bite. Mouth opening wide.

Lena swings the hammer upwards with a grunt. Claw first. The forked spike finds its mark in the beast's right eye, shattering socket and reducing eyeball to mush. Blood and gunk spew forth and soil her shoulder.

The zombie shrinks away with something like a scream. With the tool still embedded in its face, it thrashes around on top of the box, its exposed skin squeaking on the cellophane wrap.

At first Lena makes to run. But she's watched a lot of horror movies and seen too many heroes punished for not finishing off the enemy.

Bracing herself, she returns to the thing she's just hit. It's quivering as though it's in the grip of a seizure. The body once belonged to a young man, a blue collar worker barely out of his teens. Now it's a parody of humanity.

Eyes slitted, Lena pulls the hammer free, raises it high, turns it one hundred and eighty degrees and, aiming for the forehead, brings the blunt side down with force. She repeats the action twice, ignoring the crunch of bone, squelch of brain and spurting blood.

What the fuck have I become? She vomits, then dry wretches several times.

She's halfway over the next wall when the sat-phone rings in her pocket. *Of all the times to forget to put your phone on silent...* She panics; she's not sure exactly how sensitive the zombies' hearing is, and she can't tell how close they are. They could be just within the walls of the next warehouse for all she knows. The last one to menace her was stealthy. So she drops the last six feet, sending a shooting pain into her right ankle, though nothing breaks.

She doesn't recognise the number. "Hello?" she whispers.

"Adderley, it's Villeneuve." The MP's tone is all-business. "Have to use a different number, not sure if the last was secure. Have you located Lunt and Anderson?"

"No, I can't reach either."

"Okay, never mind. I have bad news, I'm afraid. This little outbreak of yours has spread."

"Spread?"

"Yes. I'm afraid so."

She swallows. *More deaths, more horror because she didn't listen to Sofia Aslam.* "Spread where? How?"

"The suburb of... Walkley. Before long, it'll be in the city of Manchester itself, according to our intelligence." A metropolis with a population of close to six hundred thousand, yet still the Member of Parliament talks as though discussing the cricket. "The vehicle crash on the... A9015 is where it began. Concentrated chemicals apparently, the escaped gas spread by high winds. Plus the treatments that have already been distributed."

"There has to be something we can do..."

"Not unless you know a way of changing the weather, Adderley. The forecast is a prevailing west to east wind, and if it's correct, Manchester will be infected by... roughly nine o'clock."

"Can't we distribute the antidote inhalers? There's a stock of thousands —"

"— Sadly not. No time. Besides, the infection is contagious via bite. Though many of the zombies seem content to mill around your factory, it appears a significant portion have wanderlust. Walkley isn't the only area nearby to have reported outbreaks."

We caused Armageddon. The whole world is going to end. Lena stands in the drizzle, pinching the bridge of her nose, breathing raggedly. Lena rues the day she met the slimy MP. He should've done his own due diligence on Resurrex, but the opposite was true. Villeneuve was just as keen to broker the contract as Evolve were to accept it, presumably to impress his Department of Environment, Food and Rural

Affairs superiors and win votes for a Conservative government under pressure to 'fix' the ecological crisis.

Villeneuve clears his throat. "Lena, are you still there?" For the first time, there's something other than disdain in his manner.

"Yes, Gordon." Her tone is bitter. "Still here."

"So that's the bad news. But here comes the *really* bad news."

"Go on."

"You need to forget about saving your company. Forget about everything apart from severing the link between Evolve and Her Majesty's Government. There needs to be no trace, do you understand? Nothing left that can expose our arrangement. It's all about confidentiality now."

"And what if I don't?"

"Pardon me?"

"What if I say 'fuck you, Gordon' and 'fuck your government'?"

"That would be unwise."

"Yeah? Well, this whole thing is pretty 'unwise', isn't it? Thousands are going to die, for fucksake."

"Probably," Villeneuve says guardedly, "but they will be the last."

"What do you mean?" Lena blinks rainwater away as she moves under a smoking shelter.

"I'll be blunt. In just under six hours, there will be a missile attack on Mortborough, one which will destroy the zombie threat, but also the whole town itself, and some of the surrounding districts. The media will be told that terrorists are to blame."

The rain drums on the perspex above Lena's head. For a few seconds, it falls more heavily, and then it lessens in intensity. *The whole town itself.*

"However, if you and your friends Lunt and Anderson can satisfactorily erase any evidence of government involvement in the development of Resurrex, before midnight, we can cancel the strike. We hope —."

"— You fucking bastards!"

"Sorry?"

"You're going to wipe a British city off the map just to save your skins?"

"No, you cretin. Not *just* to save our skins. Operation Peterloo will also stop the plague spreading. It'll save the whole fucking country!"

"Bullshit!" Lena spits. "You said that if I get rid of the link between us and you, the missiles won't be launched. If you don't launch, how do we stop the plague spreading?"

"We'll have more time… more options," he stutters. "We can… if the Government is in the clear, we can treat it differently. You don't understand —"

"— Save it, Gordon. I understand perfectly. I have five and three quarter hours to stop you nuking my city. Thanks for the heads-up." She ends the call.

Chapter 15 — Connor Norman — 18:20

He instantly regrets puffing on his inhaler. The chemicals trigger another coughing fit, which he muffles with the crook of his right arm. Connor knows he needs to keep taking the medication, though. His friends would probably call him crazy, but he reckons the vapour is stopping him becoming one of the monsters.

That's if I ever see m' friends again. Or m' mum.

Tears streak his sooty cheeks. Starting the blaze in the garage almost choked him to death – though peculiarly, his throat is no longer sore – but it helped him escape the zombies. Somehow the fumes, heat and flames seemed to disorient them. As if they were scared of the house fire, like normal people would be.

Once he'd got Bud's front door open, Connor ran for at least five minutes. Killer freaks gave chase, but he found a skateboard on Chaucer Avenue. His lungs, irritated by smoke particles, were burning by that point. Luckily, a downward slope took him and his new wheels as far as The Ox and Cart pub, where a roadblock forced him to stop. The undead were on the other side of the row of wrecked cars, but they didn't see him dash into the library. He hopes not, anyway…

They didn't, dumb-ass. I've been 'ere hours now. If they knew I was 'ere, they'd 'ave come lookin' fer me.

Still, if he *does* keeps spluttering away like an old man, they *will* hear him. They *will* break through the doors, smash the bookcases out of the way, and they *will* eat him alive. How does he stop himself from coughing, though?

Water hasn't helped. He took a bottle from the dead librarian, watching her blood-soaked body as he rummaged through her handbag. She didn't come back to life. She still hasn't. Yet. Maybe she's been mauled too badly to resurrect. Connor only glanced at her face earlier, but it looked like she'd been attacked by a bear – he almost threw up.

He stops looking at his own reflection in the window and focusses instead on the middle-distance. Five minutes ago, he saw someone in The Ox and Cart's car park. A small redheaded person, and not an undead man-eater, either. They were hiding, or trying to hide, and the dead don't hide. They find people who aren't good enough at hiding.

Am I good enough at hiding?

The answer is probably no. Seeking refuge in Mortborough's 'Community Learning Zone' was by no means a bad idea, as its multitude of portable bookcases are excellent for blocking the door. But the secret to zombie hide-and-seek is not to stay in the same place for too long.

Therefore, with that in mind, Connor will watch the road for another five minutes, and then he will leave via the fire exit. It will be more hazardous outside, obviously, but he's tired of the library anyway. Although there's only one corpse present, it smells like more. He craves fresh air.

He's under no illusions, though; he knows he's too young to survive on his own, so once he's checked out The Ox's car park, he's going to try to find his father. Dad's office is a couple of miles away, which means a journey of approximately half an hour if Connor hurries. If he encounters any other kids, like the one he saw a moment ago, he'll invite them to join him. They can be a team and look out for each other. That's the plan.

Or, I walk outside, 'n' a stinkin', 'ungry zombie grabs me before I can even get on the skateboard.

Safe havens like the learning zone are a precious commodity in Mortborough, so Connor does not clear the entryway to make his exit. He might want to come back if his next excursion goes awry. After saying a quick prayer to a god who seems to have taken a day off, he slips out of the window in the disabled toilets. He lands in cat faeces.

Good start, numb-nuts.

As he emerges from the terrace behind the library, he looks left, right, left, right. Gladstone Road is empty. He dashes to the junction with Chaucer, staying low. Once he's around the corner, he can see the pub's parking lot. There's no child there, though. So he crosses the street to investigate, keeping an eye on the roadblock as he goes. All of the crazies that were congregating around the cars earlier are gone.

The pub's big doors are firmly shut, the windows unbroken. Next Connor looks down the ginnel that runs between the convenience shop and The Ox. At the end of the alleyway, there are four recycling bins, each one with a different coloured lid. He sees no one, hears nothing, but he can *sense* something.

Is it one of them?

No, of course not; a zombie would be at his throat by now. Just when Connor's about to dismiss his sixth sense as childishness, the 'something' moves. One of the bins rocks. Somebody's behind them, against the brick wall of the flats behind the pub. They're whispering.

Connor creeps down the ginnel, avoiding the larger pools of water among the cobbles. He can hear his heartbeat in his ears. Sweat pinpricks his upper lip. "Hello?"

There's a sudden buzz of hushed conversation. Then a girl – cute, ginger, freckled and about nine years of age – appears. "Hi," she says. "Who are you?"

"Connor. You?"

"Bea."

"Who's that with you?"

"Err… no one."

The boy folds his arms. "Don't fib. I 'eard ya talkin' t' someone."

"Okay." Bea turns away. "Come on, kids."

All four bin lids fly open, giving Connor a palpitation. The plastic containers wobble and butt against each other as a pair of boys and a pair of girls climb out. They share introductions: brunette Evie has just turned nine and is about six months younger than Bea. Blonde-haired Emily is eight, as is coffee-skinned Reece, and tiny Muhammed is barely five.

I'm the oldest. I need t' look after these kids, 'cause they don't stand a chance on their own. Yeah, Bea's done a good job so far, but stayin' 'round 'ere's a mistake.

Their stories are similar to Connor's. None actually saw their mums or dads killed, which, on reflection, has probably saved their lives, for the shock of witnessing their parents' demise would render most children catatonic.

Connor doesn't say as much, but he reckons they're all orphans. They're in denial, hoping their loved ones will come and find them and everything will return to normal.

Hang on a sec. Am I *in denial? Is looking for* my *dad pointless?*

It takes five minutes to persuade the younger kids to leave the ginnel.

"Where we goin'?" Bea asks. She's the most vocal.

"Well," Connor says, crouching behind one of cars making up the roadblock. "*I'm* goin' t' find my dad. He works at Union Energy, couple o' miles away. You lot don't 'ave t' come wi' me, though. It'll prob'ly be dangerous."

To his surprise, they *do* want to accompany him. And although the added responsibility of five younger children bothers Connor at first, he enjoys a sense of satisfaction. He's helping people more vulnerable than him. They're relying on him to make the right decision. Plus, they're a pleasant bunch: polite, respectful and obedient, though that could be due to fear and stress.

Their faith in him is tested after ten minutes of walking in the rain. When Chaucer Avenue crosses Delamere Road, they turn left, but the sight of oncoming undead in the distance prompts them to take a shortcut through Windsor Gardens. As they slip into the park, splashing through puddles, Connor thinks he hears the sound of a car. He's too anxious about the zombies to stop and check.

The recreational area is more of a broad parade than a park: a single path with anorexic trees to either side. To the right of the walkway, at the opposite end to Delamere in an area clear of trees, there's a playground. Closer by, on the left, lies a small skatepark that Connor's visited once or twice. Its half-pipe, ramps and bowl are haunted by a group of zombies.

Luckily, Muhammed has eyes like a hawk, and he spots the undead skater-boys and skater-girls from a distance of fifty yards; he also sees movement on the playground in the distance. The kids duck behind a water feature.

"Crap." Connor looks at Bea, who's adopted the role of his deputy. "You reckon we follow the fence on the right, stay in the trees, 'n' get past 'em that way?"

Bea purses rosy lips. "Maybe. But there's zombies on the playground, too. We'll be walkin' right into 'em."

"Good point." *The kids are all watchin' me. Expectin' me to come up with somethin'. We could turn back. But there's zombies on Delamere now. Come on, dumb-ass, think.*

Suddenly, he's reminded of a mission in an Xbox game. The setting is weirdly-similar to level 5 of 'Global Warfare', and if he remembers correctly, there was only one way of getting past the aliens to the safehouse.

"Right. 'Ere's what we do. Bea, you take Emily 'n' Reece down the right. Don't worry about bein' 'eard or spotted. Make plenty o' noise. They'll spot ya —"

"— They'll catch us!" Reece interjects. "They're fast, remember."

"Yeah, but they're clumsy too. They won't be so fast in all these trees 'n' bushes. Anyway. Me, Evie 'n' little Mo will go down the left when the zombies have been distracted into chasin' you guys. Then we do the same thing on our side. We distract the ones on the playground while you go down the right."

He has to explain the strategy one more time, but his young charges are smart. Hopefully, they won't freeze under pressure.

His hands are shaking, his mouth dry. "Ready?"

Bea, twenty yards away, nods. "Ready."

"Go!"

She and her two companions break into a run. They dodge between the skeletal trees, making as much of a din as they can. As expected, the skater-zombs lurch towards the trio.

"Now!" Connor leads the charge. He hurdles shrubs and patches of mud, with Mo and Evie close behind. "Keep goin'!" he yells as they near the playground. His stomach churns when, for the briefest of moments, he makes eye contact with a middle-aged male zombie crossing the path, but it collides with a tree.

Soon enough, both halves of the team are past the undead. In single file, they race out of Windsor Gardens, to safety.

"I think it's left here," Connor says, leading the group down Juniper Street and into a council estate.

"My mum grew up 'ere," Bea states as they pass the first shattered bus shelter. "Now she won't even drive through it."

"Why?" asks Evie.

"Something to do with drugs."

"Doesn't look that bad t' me." Reece shrugs. "Apart from the smashed windows 'n' that, but that's 'cause o' the zombies, innit?"

Connor steps over a large pool of blood next to a crashed car. "One of my mates lives 'round 'ere. He goes to a different school, though. His mum 'n' mine —"

"— Shh," says little Muhammed. "I can hear somethin'."

They stop and take cover behind the battered SUV.

Timid Emily says, "It's a car. Maybe someone's come to save us —"

"— Shut up!" Connor feels bad for silencing her, because she's barely spoken so far, but he too can hear a vehicle approaching. It sounds like a big one. He risks a peek over the bonnet of the Jeep: about a quarter of a football field away, up ahead, a white Ford van, driving slowly, is turning left onto Juniper Street. "It's coming this way."

Although the others look delighted, Connor feels inexplicably wary. "Stay down. Maybe it'll pass us by."

His comrades look at him in confusion.

"They might be 'ere to rescue us," Bea suggests.

"Yeah," Evie says, "it might be the police, or somethin'."

"The police'd be in a police car," Connor's maintains. "If it's a normal person, they might've been bitten. Which means they could turn at any time."

"Bein' bitten might not even make people turn." Bea argues. "We don't know that's true for sure. And we don't even know if they have been bitten. They might just be normal —"

"— Just stay down 'n' be quiet, all o' ya." Connor's tone is harsh now.

Barely faster than walking pace, the Transit passes. As it trundles past, the kids circle around the 4x4, keeping it between them and the moving vehicle.

Then little Mo runs in the opposite direction.

"Shit." Connor is torn. If he chases after Muhammed, he might be seen by the van driver. If he doesn't, the driver might see Mo. Or he might see them anyway.

What now? Maybe I'm bein' paranoid; maybe we should just let 'em rescue us.

The van rolls to a stop. Its engine revs as it reverses.

They've seen Mo. Should I leave 'im to get caught, 'n' look after everyone else, or should I try t' protect 'im? He is the smallest, 'n' I'm the biggest.

Once more, the Ford Transit stops, but this time with a screech of brakes.

"What should we do?" whispers Bea, her face now pale.

Good question. What would Trent or Dad do?

The van door opens and closes a moment later. A man is talking, but his words are just a rumble at this distance. Mo might be answering; he might not. He's too far away to know.

Screw it.

Connor stands. He's an inch shy of five feet in height, though he feels much shorter at the moment.

The van man, who has a hand on Mo's shoulder, notices Connor and waves. "Hi," he calls. His face is pallid, his hair and moustache the colour of copper. He looks vaguely familiar.

Connor returns the adult's smile as he approaches, wondering why he looks so nervous. *Surely I should be the scared one?*

"Hi." The man, leading Mo, stops five yards short of the crashed SUV. "I'm Gary. You're Connor, right?"

"Yeah." The boy frowns. *How does he know m' name? Maybe Mo told 'im.*

"I work with your dad."

"Where is he?"

"At my house. He's really worried about you —"

"— So why's he not out lookin' fer me?"

"He's hurt his leg, so he's laid up. I said I'd keep an eye out for you while I was lookin' for my son."

"What's your son's name?"

"What?" Gary's smile wavers. "Oh, he's called Billy."

Connor bites his lip. "Right."

"I found Billy. He's in the van, and I was just on my way back home when I saw your little friend here. But I think Billy's been bitten."

"Oh, that sucks…"

"Yeah. I'm gonna take him home, but I'll need some help carryin' him in the house. You look like a strong lad. If you come back with me, you can see your dad, and help me with Billy."

This seems… weird. Is Dad really at this guy's 'ouse? He does look familiar, so maybe I've seen 'im on my dad's Facebook, or somethin'.

"Oh, hi." Gary's looking past Connor now.

Bea, Evie and Reece have revealed themselves. They're moving to join their de facto leader as he follows Gary to his van. When they're all stood alongside the vehicle, its owner opens the sliding side door. A boy, barely visible in the gloom, is lying down on a strip of carpet. He's roughly the same age as Connor.

"Get in, will you," Gary says. "Billy's out cold, but it'll be good for him to see friendly faces when he comes 'round."

Looking relieved, Bea, Evie and Reece climb inside.

Connor hesitates. *Hang on, why's he keepin' 'is son in the back? Why's he not up front with 'is dad?*

Behind him, a foot scrapes on asphalt. Suddenly he's being shoved into the van; he lands hard on his hands and knees. He cries out and spins onto his bottom. The last thing

129

he sees before the cargo door slams shut is Emily and Mo, running for their lives, while Connor and the other three cry out in terror.

Chapter 16 — Luke Norman — 19:35

Anderson's dead. So why are we still 'ere?

Breathing quietly, Luke steps into the castle loft's second room. The aches in his ribs and head have been exorcised by an all-encompassing compulsion to get to his boy.

Lunt said he was staying because he didn't wanna leave his mate behind. But she's bled t' death, so why the fuck are we still 'angin' 'round?

The ex-army officer is alone. Brad, whose depression seems to have worsened since the successful defence of the castle, is on the roof above. Lunt reckons he can wirelessly connect his standard mobile phone to the satellite dish, a trick he was apparently shown by some Russian fellow. Brad agreed to assist and is tampering with the satellite dish outside.

Why's Brad 'elpin' the man who's keepin' us prisoner, anyway? He wasn't this spineless when he was shootin' all those zombies from the wall. But he was doin' as he was told then, too. Grief's turned 'im into a shell of a man. Maybe that's what I'll be like when I find Connor dead or undead…

No. Luke can't think like that; he needs to focus on escaping so he can find his child, who is still alive. The next step on that journey will probably be the hardest, and it'll be taken here. Only one thing, one *man*, can stand in his way. Unfortunately, said obstacle is at least six foot three and weighs somewhere between nineteen and twenty stone. *'N' he's trained t' kill with his bare hands.*

The soldier is distracted, though, fiddling with his phone. Luke almost got the better of the Scotsman during the fracas outside; this time *he'll* have the element of surprise on his side. As long as Lunt doesn't look up and catch the younger man taking his gun from the top of the storage chest...

Just three more steps. The floorboards are old up here, and one creaks as Luke lays his hand on the Glock.

"Yer good," Lunt says without turning in his chair. "No' many can sneak up on me like that."

Luke lifts the pistol, clicks the safety switch and aims at the big man's head. "Don't move." A joist is partially-blocking his line of fire, so he sidesteps to the right.

"I won't. I'm no' daft."

"We're leavin'."

"Aye? What do yer friends say?"

"They'll come wi' me."

"But ye've no' asked 'em yet."

"No."

"Brad seems tae like helpin' me."

"Brad's not 'imself. He's up 'n' down, he has been all day. If you asked 'im 'alf an hour earlier or later, he'd probably have said 'no'. He 'ad to kill 'is own undead kid, for fucksake."

"He's had a rough time. Bein' somewhere safe, like this castle, would be good fer him."

Luke is armed; he holds all the power. For some reason, however, he wants to justify his actions. "I've got a son. I need t' try 'n' find 'im. Then we're leavin' town 'n' goin' to m' dad's farm."

"Right ye are." Lunt looks up at the open skylight at the sound of a rustle then a bang from the roof. For the first time, he meets Luke's gaze. His blue eyes are cold, dispassionate. "So what ye waitin' for?"

"Nothin'. Be goin' soon. But why are *you* stayin', Lunt?"

"Ah need to get m' phone workin'.'"

"Yeah, but I mean, why not just leave town altogether?"

"Ah have orders."

Luke swaps the Glock to his other hand to wipe sweat from his palm. "It can't just be that." *Why am I tryin' t' reason with 'im? Just get out now, while ya can.* "Is it somethin' t' do wi' that 'Lena' you mentioned to Anderson?"

The older fellow blows air from his nostrils. "Maybe. Women are m' weakness, always have been. Anyway, good luck tae ye, son. I still think ye should stay here, but."

"Why?"

"Soon enough, a taskforce'll be sent, 'n' they won't be a rescue outfit. They'll be serious. They'll make the zombies look like pussycats."

"All the more reason fer me to find my boy."

"Aye, fair dues. I can see I'm no' gonnae persuade ye tae see sense. But be careful out there, Luke. Me 'n' Anderson got sloppy. Shit, if it weren't for me bein' soft, ye'd be dead already. But the taskforce won't be sentimental auld men like me. They won't take prisoners."

"Okay."

"Where's the lassie?"

"I left her asleep. I didn't want 'er gettin' 'urt, if things went bad between me 'n' you."

"Love during the apocalypse. What a cliché."

Luke feigns bemusement. "It's not love… it's not anything."

Lunt raises his eyebrows. "Right ye are. Well, you 'n' her'll have some alone time together now."

"How do ya mean?"

"Yer buddy Brad's stayin' here wi' me. I need his IT skills."

"No way. I'm not leavin' 'im behind."

"Yes, ye are."

Keeping the handgun trained on its owner, Luke approaches the stepladder placed under the skylight.

Lunt is up like a shot. He reaches for the window handle, pulls it closed with a thud and extricates the key from the lock.

Both men disregard Brad's muffled protests from outside. They stand ten feet from one another.

Luke points the gun at Lunt's forehead. "Gimme the key."

"No." The burly warrior rolls his shoulders. "Come 'n' get it."

"I'll fire."

"No ye won't."

He's right. I can't shoot 'im in cold blood fer defyin' me, 'n' Lunt knows that. He knows I'm not cut from the same cloth as 'im 'n' Anderson. "Right. Fuck you, then." Luke doesn't have to kill anyone. Instead, he'll lock his former incarcerator in the attic before going outside to find another way of getting Brad back to terra firma. He backs away from the Scot while keeping the man's shaven head in the Glock's sights.

Until his right heel and calf hit something solid. He only loses balance for a moment, but the base of the diagonal beam causes enough of a stumble for Lunt to capitalise. The giant covers the distance between them at a frightening speed. Rushing then leaping like a tiger, he barrels into Luke's midriff just as the latter recovers his footing.

Suddenly, the smaller man's lungs are empty. He panics. He truly believes for an instant that he'll never breathe again. Then the floor swings up to whack him. It simultaneously smashes his rump, his shoulder blades and the back of his head. He's blind. Then a column of stone, the sort one might find in the Colosseum, falls upon him. A second, thinner slab is across his throat. He's trapped between wood and rock. He's being asphyxiated.

It's not a rock, ya dick. It's Lunt. He's got ya pinned down, 'n' he's stranglin' ya with 'is forearm.

The fog clears from Luke's sight as adrenaline floods his blood. Lunt's big, meaty face is inches from his own, so he reaches up and pokes at an eye.

The Scotsman grunts in pain. In arching away to avoid gouging fingers, he lessens the pressure on the Englishman's windpipe. By using his left hand to grab said digits, the chokehold weakens further.

Luke gasps for air, squirms desperately to shift the other man's bulk, grabs at the sapling-thick arm at his neck with his left hand, wriggles the fingers of his right in Lunt's bear-like paw, gasps for air, squirms desperately...

Now Luke's mangled right hand is free.

But so is Lunt's left.

It comes down as a fist, like a hammer on an anvil.

Darkness with a shower of stars. Liquid iron in his mouth. There's something Luke has to do, someone he has to fight, somebody to save, but the concepts are as intangible as the cosmos sprinkling his mind's eye.

The weight is lifting, and he feels suddenly light, as though he can fly away. Is he dead? Have the angels come to claim him?

No, ya prick. That fat bastard Lunt's climbed off ya. Those bumps are 'is footsteps, 'cause he's goin' t' get the gun ya dropped when ya tripped up like a fuckin' mong.

Luke has to get up. He needs to get out of here, find Connor and get out of Mortborough. Brad can stay here, Jada too. As long as he can locate his son, nothing else matters.

He can only see the rafters above, which means he's still on his back. Sitting up hurts; everything is painful. Standing is worse, and he fears losing control of his stomach. Lunt is wobbling in his vision.

"Give up, Luke." The soldier's gruff voice comes from the left, but Lunt is directly in front. The big man's reaching out to him, as if to help, so Luke moves towards him. "Laddie, I'm pointin' a fuckin' pistol at yer head. Stay where ye are. Jesus wept. Mustae hit ye too hard."

Lunt isn't offering a helping hand. As explained, he's aiming a Glock 21 at his foe, who's finally regaining his wits.

"Shit." Luke thumbs blood from tender lips. He steadies himself against a support beam and stares at his conqueror with a weary animosity. "Ya kicked my arse."

"Aye. But it wasnae easy. Don't wannae hurt you, Luke, but ah need ye tae stand down now. Sit down, preferably."

Accepting the invitation, Luke all but collapses onto the storage chest.

Wind whistles outside. There's a noise from the roof window, a tapping against glass. Brad's still up there, and he probably wants to get out of the storm.

"I just wanna see m' son."

"I know, kid. 'N' ye will, eventually. Wait here a minute. I'm just gonnae go get ye some water." The former army officer goes into the loft's first room.

A thud is quickly followed by a screech of pure agony.

Chapter 17 — Jada Blakowska — 19:40

The crunch of metatarsal is sickening. Hanging onto the loft ladder, she raises the rolling pin again, but this time she brings it down onto solid timber, jarring her arm – Lunt moved his size 13 foot. He hops away, cursing.

She pulls herself through the trapdoor. Luke heads her way, his face a mask of blood. Lunt's limping with his back to her, and he's raising his pistol. Just as he fires, Luke reaches him and pushes his gun hand aside. Glass shatters somewhere in the attic's other room. The two men brawl, both injured, both refusing to surrender.

Bludgeon held high, Jada blindsides Lunt. He twists aside at the last second, though. The pin glances off his wrist, knocking the pistol from his hand, then catching Luke's left elbow before it slips from her grasp. The younger man yelps. A gut punch doubles him over; a knee snaps his head back.

But as he sinks to his knees, Luke hammers at Lunt's wounded instep.

The older man roars in anguish.

Jada jumps on his massive back.

Again Luke pounds Lunt's foot, but this time he misses. A double-handed blow to the top of his head puts him down.

The big guy easily pries the woman's arm from his neck. He shakes her loose as a buffalo would a hyena.

She lands awkwardly; a needle of pain jabs her ankle.

Oh, fuck, that's sore. Hang on, was that a bump in the other room?

Still flat on his face, Luke moans.

Lunt, panting, leans on a joist as his eyes scan the floor. He's looking for his gun, and if he finds it, Jada's time will be up. "Fuck," he mutters, shuffling towards the other half of the loft space. When he reaches the doorway, he stops.

There's a thud, like a cricket bat hitting a ball. The agent staggers backwards. He puts too much weight on his bad foot and crashes to the floorboards.

Brad appears, a silhouette against the light in the attic's back chamber, with a mallet in one hand.

But like some sort of indestructible cyborg, Captain Harry Lunt is rising to his feet. Although blood streams from a cut to his bald pate, he seems unconcerned. He puts a hand out to Brad and gives him the 'bring it on' gesture.

The rolling pin, where's the rolling pin? Jada's eyes flicker from one dark corner to the next. And that's when she sees the black metal of the Glock 21. While Lunt hobbles towards a dwarfed Brad, the journalist pushes herself into a crouch then lunges. She seizes the handgun as she lands on her hip. Ignoring the stab of pain, she swings the weapon to bear on the behemoth about to destroy Brad. "Stop!" she screams. *Please, just fuckin' stop!* "I've got your gun."

All the fight leaves Lunt. He sinks to his knees, head bowed, his deep chest rising and falling. Rising and falling.

"Luke?" Brad croaks. "You okay, bro?"

"Not really, mate." Luke rolls onto his back and, whimpering, pushes himself into a sitting position. "I 'urt everywhere. Jada, you alright?"

She blinks. Suddenly the Glock is too heavy in her hand, so she lets it drop to her lap while keeping the barrel aimed at Lunt. "I'm alive."

"I'm good, in case you were interested," says Brad. "Cut my hand, but it's not bad. Did it climbin' through the skylight. That gunshot smashed it. I reckon I finished fixing the dish up, anyway."

Luke smiles wryly. "So Lunt woulda let ya go. We fought for nothin'."

The Scotsman in question doesn't confirm or deny his opponent's assumption, nor does he speak when he has his hands bound.

The three friends lock Lunt in the loft before going to one of the bathrooms to dress wounds. They use their inhalers, then collect the guns and ammunition, along with some food, water and first aid equipment, plus an assortment of tools and knives.

There's a jalopy of a hatchback outside the castle, a VW Golf. It won't start. They therefore head for the closest park exit on foot. The evening is warm, wet and prematurely dark. Thunder rumbles. Lightning flashes. There's a miasma of decay in the air, as if the whole town of Mortborough has died and risen. Jada's ankle is a throbbing inferno. She hopes it's a sprain only, but even if it isn't fractured, it'll need rest it's unlikely to get.

The main thoroughfare is alive with the dead, most of which are travelling in the same direction as the humans. Sticking to the emaciated trees that run parallel with the roadway, treading as lightly as they can, they avoid the zombies that have wandered away from the herd. Firearms remain holstered or strapped to backs, for firing them will only draw attention. Twice they have to break into a run to escape the more curious or alert amongst the undead.

The group are silent, their faces neutral.

I should be traumatised. The things I've seen, the mayhem on the dual carriageway, the mechanic, the woman killin' the boy in the street, all the zombies I shot at the castle, the brawl with Lunt. We should all be fucked in the head. But we're not. We're just ploddin' along, dodgin' man-eating psychos. Our only thought is survival.

So much for Jacobia with Gracie. Fine Colombian coffee and smoked salmon have been traded for murderous ghouls and gun-toting mercenaries. There is, though, a part of Jada that relishes the new world into which she's been plunged. She's always been an adrenaline junkie. The excitement of her short stint in the Army Reserve, which ended due to a messy break-up with her childhood sweetheart, was only partly replaced by her career as a reporter. Investigative journalism can be exhilarating; it can also be dull.

Warrencroft's exit is just about visible in the gloom, as is the horde thronging the way out. Their numbers are concentrated into a bottleneck.

"Looks like we're climbin' the fence, then," Brad says.

They arc their approach to arrive at the perimeter about seventy yards from the zombie mass. The trees are thicker on the edge of the park, the ground more boggy.

Jada's shoes are sodden by the time she reaches the twelve feet high railings.

"We could use the trees t' climb over." Luke's voice is nasal, for his nose was flattened by Lunt's knee. He's still handsome, though. *And brave, and determined to reach his son, and just the right age for me… Jesus, get a grip, Jada.*

Brad's the first to attempt the ascent, but he puts too much weight on the elm's rotten limb. Wood cracks; splinters fall, followed by Brad himself. He falls with a yell and lands with a thump.

"Jesus, mate," Luke hisses, helping his friend to his feet. "Be quiet!"

"Thanks for the concern, bro." The shorter man nurses his left arm. "Fuckin' 'urts like fuck."

"We'll kiss it better, if ya just be quiet."

Jada's already looking away, at the multitude of monsters gathered around the gate. "It's too late for that."

"Eh?" Brad is flexing the fingers of his right hand.

"They've already heard us."

Jada might be overreacting a little, because not *all* of the zombies are breaking away from the pack. Only twenty or so. The fiends are hurrying towards the survivors, bumping into trees and sliding in puddles in their desperation to feast.

"Shit." Luke checks his pistols. "We shoot 'em, 'n' the rest'll hear. Then we'll be fucked."

"Too many to fight hand-to-hand," Brad observes.

"We need to get over." Jada grabs one of the fence's bars. "It's the only option. Luke, we'll boost Brad up."

They do so.

"Now pull up Luke."

"What, that fat bastard?" Brad is straddling the top of the railings.

The enemy are thirty yards away.

"Just do it! He can stand on my back, too." She drops to all fours.

Luke hesitates. "What about you?"

"I'm lighter, so I can use the trees. Just get on!" She winces as he stands on her spine. The load disappears as, between himself and Brad, Luke is dragged to the summit.

Fifteen yards and closing. She can see the zombies' facial features now, the gouges and chipped teeth, the muck and gore on their clothes.

Gripping the head height tree branch stops her fingers from trembling. It feels strong enough, though it creaks when she uses its support to haul her feet to a lower limb.

"Come on, Jada!" Luke and Brad shout.

Five yards.

The fastest freak, a child, misses her thigh by a whisker as she lifts herself higher. The second isn't to be foiled, however. It snags her sore ankle; she gasps.

Oh fuck oh no!

The once-female creature below wrenches and pulls. Its blood-blackened teeth are already snapping. A curious keening emanates from its mouth. By wrapping her right arm around a thicker branch and lacing the fingers of both hands together, Jada manages to resist.

"Pull, Jada!" Luke screams.

Zombie three, a hard-hatted former builder, is taller and heavier. It'll pluck her down like a ripe orange.

She closes her eyes.

A strong hand seizes her knee.

Then there's a gunshot, and the grip slackens. Three, four, five more whip-cracks, then a ragged volley. Wallops as lead punctures flesh, the rustle of bullets through trees and plants. Undead bodies hit the floor.

They saved me knowin' they'd alert the horde in the process and put themselves in more danger.

Tears dampen Jada's eyes as she continues to scale the tree. Before long she's high enough to reach the fence top, so she swings onto the steel.

"Come on," Luke urges from below. "I'll catch you."

She drops into his arms. He fumbles, and she slips to the pavement, but he took the force out of her descent.

Twin lines of ugly, dead cannibals – one within the park's grounds, the other outside – are streaming their way. So they run into nearby housing estate, a perfect place to lose the brainless creatures. By the time Jada, Luke and Brad reach the opposite side, their hunters are have been left behind. Her ankle is on fire, her gait awkward.

They're now at Mortborough Bus Depot. It seems as good a place as any to rest and take stock, so they break into the bus company's offices and slip into the staff room. Tools are used to breach the vending machines. Plastic seats offer tired legs much-needed respite. There's a musty smell, but it's that of unemptied bins, not rotting flesh. At least it's dry, too.

"So where now?" Brad doesn't seem as distraught as he was earlier, thankfully. Adrenaline and testosterone are keeping grief at bay, for now.

"Connor." Luke's face is bruised, his hair matted with blood. But he's relentless. "I need t' find Connor." He pauses and gives Jada a smile. "If that's okay with you? I mean, we're just, like, draggin' you 'round everywhere with us. Not even askin' if yer cool with it."

"Well," she says, clicking her tongue. "I don't have family here at the moment."

"Me neither," says Brad. "Not now. My mum 'n' dad 'n' brothers live in London."

"What's keepin' you goin', then?"

"Helpin' Luke. I might've lost my kid, but if I can 'elp 'im find Connor, at least some good'll come of all this shit."

"Thanks, mate. Appreciate it." Luke squeezes his friend's shoulder. "But Jada, there must be somethin' that's important to ya."

"I guess. I think I know who's responsible for this —"

"— The zombies?" Luke and Brad say in unison.

"Yeah. And I wanna expose 'em."

"Fuckin' right," says Brad. "Who is it?"

She shares her suspicions. When she's done, the fatigue on the men's faces has been replaced by anger, which they voice with a healthy side of expletives.

"It's crucial they're held accountable. Not just so justice can be done. But because we need to make sure nothin' like this ever happens again."

Luke's fists bunch. "Never again."

"They killed my fuckin' daughter!" Brad slams the break table with the edge of his uninjured hand. "Not the zombies, the fuckin' corporations 'n' politicians." His top lip quivers. "They'll fuckin' pay fer this."

Nostrils flaring, Jada nods. "But your Connor's more important than any of that. We'll save him, then worry about screwin' over Evolve. And the Government."

Luke looks relieved. "So, like, climate change caused a zombie apocalypse?"

"Bit of an over-simplification, but yeah, I guess."

"Shit. Anyway, we need to make a move. But we can't just be wanderin' 'round town. We need a quicker, but safer, way o' gettin' about."

"If it's a vehicle, it'll be noisy. So it needs t' be tough." Brad snorts. "A tank'd do it."

"Or a bus." Jada tips her forehead at the sheltered forecourt outside. "Like one of those out there."

Finding the ignition keys is easy; they're kept in a store room next to the canteen. In his early twenties, Luke drove the minibus for his pub football team, so he'll take the wheel. They choose a single-decker which looks to have been repaired recently. With a wheeze, its double doors open. Luke steps aboard, as does Brad.

Jada freezes, however. To their rear, someone has just cocked a gun.

"Going somewhere, kids?" The man's voice is educated. "Don't turn around. Don't move a fucking muscle. Not if you want to keep your brains *inside* your skulls, instead of splattered all over my bus."

She can feel Luke and Brad tense, though they're as motionless as commanded.

Fucking hell, we were just startin' to get somewhere.

Chapter 18 — Connor Norman — 9pm

They've got me. The zombies 'ave killed me! This must be hell, *but I've always been a good boy. Why would I be in 'ell?*

The truth is that Connor's not one of the damned, he realises as he blinks grit from gummed-up eyes. He's woken up somewhere strange. A dim, confined space, but not a subterranean world of smoke, lava and demons.

As his eyes adjust to the gloom, he realises he's in a box bedroom. The only light is that of a streetlight outside. The window's blind covers all but two inches of the glass. This room is bare, furniture free, the only feature a lamp on the floor. Its flex is cut, the plug absent, so he's stuck in the dark for now.

How long has he been unconscious? *Shit. My inhaler! I'm gonna turn into one of* them*! Thank god, it's still in my pocket.*

He takes his medicine, coughs, then sits up and groans, for his back and neck are stiff from lying on the hard floor. He stands. His knees shake for an instant, and he feels faint, though the sensation soon passes. Ears straining, he hears nothing, no movement elsewhere in the house or flat, or whatever.

A slamming sound from below sets his heart racing. And silence again. The building Connor's in is at least two-storey, then, unless the noise came from a basement.

They always 'ave basements in American movies, don't they? We don't 'ave many over —

Another bang, followed by a scream, that of a child. He suddenly recalls that he's not alone now; he has Bea and the others to consider. They're all kids, while he's practically a teenager. It sounds like one of them is in trouble downstairs, being chased by a zombie, perhaps.

Or maybe it's Gary. The adult's face flashes before the boy's mind's eye as clearly as a photograph. Connor didn't trust him as soon as he saw his bony hand on Muhammed's shoulder, but he doubted his own instincts. He won't make the same mistake again, he resolves.

I might not get the chance. Who knows what Gary's got planned fer me? I might wind up dead, like Billy, in the back o' the van.

A girl screeches again, but this time a grown-up male answers.

After tiptoeing to the doorway, Connor presses his ear against the hard door. Although he can't make out the girl's words, the man's deeper voice carries better.

"Just — as — told. Or — be sorry — promise you."

'Just do as you're told. Or you'll be sorry, I promise you' – that's what Gary said.

What's the girl bein' told t' do, though? Is Gary a paedo? Daley Messina at school said that paedos always *kill kids once they've bummed 'em…*

"— going out — won't — long. Just shut — for — sake!"

Suddenly Connor is torn. He doesn't want to reveal he's woken up, anger Gary and invite some sort of abuse, but he hates the thought of being locked in the box room. *What if Gary doesn't come back, if he gets caught by zombs? Then I'll be stuck in 'ere. I'll never see Mum 'n' then Dad again, 'n' I'll starve t' death. The other kids'll die too.*

Should he bang on the bedroom door, or wait till Gary's gone and try to escape?

A scuffle downstairs has his pulse thundering once more. Someone's running; somebody bigger and heavier is chasing. Then there's a scream, different to the others he's heard thus far, higher-pitched.

"No, no, no!" the girl pleads.

Two thuds.

Now someone's weeping. Like an infant, but not like an infant. It's Gary, and for the briefest of moments, the imprisoned boy pities the odd fellow, until he guesses the probable reason.

He's killed the girl.

A glacial chill descends his spine as sweat trickles in the same direction.

He's killed the girl. I just hid in 'ere, like a baby, while it 'appened. 'N' it was my job t' protect these kids.

A sob escapes his throat, so he covers his mouth. Tears well, then trickle down his cheeks when he squeezes his eyes shut. He's seen dead bodies and been chased by the undead, but this is the first death he's witnessed in real time.

Downstairs, a door opens. There's a dragging sound, and a door closes. A vehicle starts outside, its engine revving as tyres squeal on tarmac. Gary's gone. Slumping to his knees, Connor breathes a sigh of relief.

But he'll be back. I need t' do somethin' fer the other kids, if they've not already been murdered.

The door handle pulls down, but the door itself won't budge. With gritted teeth, the youngster kicks the door, once, twice, thrice. All he gets for his trouble is a sore foot and leg. Once more he rattles the doorknob, even though he knows it's locked.

What kinda sicko puts locks on the outside *o' bedroom doors? There's gotta be another way out.*

The window. Connor raises the blackout blinds, letting in the paltry remnants of the day's light. The window-frame isn't uPVC like those at home; it's wooden. Like the door, the window is locked without a key. The wood is rotting, though, and the glass looks thin, as if it's not double-glazed. Spinning on his heel, he reappraises the bedroom's contents.

The lamp isn't the average, budget Ikea sort. A couple of feet high and constructed from solid metal, the appliance isn't light in Connor's hand, either. Once the shade has been prized off, its base makes short work of the window's single pane. The boy grimaces at the noise, suddenly anxious that Gary has an accomplice who's stayed in the house. He waits for ten ponderous seconds before deciding no one's heard.

Once he's swept away as much broken glass as possible, he ties the lamp's cord to his belt, climbs onto the windowsill, swings his legs out of the opening and leans back through the window to collect the lamp. He pushes himself forward, grimacing when a rogue shard of glass scores his bottom.

Now, looking left, right and down, he can see the rest of the building wall. It's not a house. In fact, he knows where he is, because his dad once stayed at this ramshackle bed-and-breakfast, a few years back. The next time Dad spent slept out after that, he didn't come back. The night breeze tickles fresh tears on the child's cheekbones.

Come on, dumbass. Now's not the time fer feelin' sorry fer yerself.

A drainpipe runs close to the window, so Connor shuffles along the ledge till he can reach the cast iron pipe. He grips the metal with his right hand, ignores the butterflies in his stomach, and pivots to grab the drainpipe with his left. Then he's in limbo. Hanging onto the downpipe like one of the daredevils he watches on YouTube. His toes teetering on a bracket. The lamp dangles beneath him, yanking at his trousers.

Luckily, the pipe is closer to the adjacent window than the one through which he's just climbed. Holding on with one arm, he reaches down with the other to retrieve the lamp. He'll have to use his left hand to smash the second window. Still, it does the trick, and more glass tinkles on the overgrown yard below.

Getting through the second window is harder, with more cuts. By now, though, Connor is pumped-up with adrenaline, full of confidence. He wipes bloody hands on his trousers and crosses the dark room to try the door. It's unlocked, but the hinges creak like something from a horror film.

Out on the dismal landing, gathered around a stairway, there are five more doorways. He doesn't bother with the first on the right, of course, because it leads to his temporary jail cell. Three of the other four open into rooms as bare as the two he's already seen. The fourth is locked, though not by key; there's a latch below the knob, which Connor unfastens. Pausing to listen in case anyone is stirring within, he can hear the thump of his own heart.

The stench assails him as soon as he opens the door. A person has died in the sixth first floor room, of that there's no doubt. Compelled to enter yet terrified of what he may meet, the kid slowly pushes the door wide. Forced to cover his nose and mouth with one hand, he reaches for the light switch. The bulb illuminates for a few seconds then sputters out. But it was on for long enough for him to see.

Connor reels away and slams the door shut behind himself. When he closes his eyes, the image of an ancient, wizened, gaunt, dead woman lay in a soiled bed returns to haunt him.

Retching, he runs down the stairs into a decrepit hallway. *I need t' find the other kids before they end up like the girl, or Billy, or the old lady upstairs.* He checks each of the candlelit rooms off the main corridor, finding old-fashioned furniture, piles of newspapers, cardboard boxes and various toys from the eighties and nineties, but no children.

Shit! Where are they? Has that nonce Gary already killed 'em?

His search ends in a grimy kitchen, where a large bloodstain on the linoleum stops him dead. For a moment he is stationary and out of breath, his fists clenching and unclenching. In the silence, he hears a sound not made by himself for the first time since Gary fled. He follows muffled cries back to the corridor, hoping to see a closet or compartment he missed.

Under the staircase there's a square in the floor. Connor drops to the wooden floor – the buzz of plaintive voices intensifies. The trapdoor has a handle, which he opens. The voices get louder, but it's too dark to see anything. Attached to the underside of the hatch is a retractable ladder like the one to his loft. It's pulled-up at the moment. Hanging from the ceiling, just inside, there's a cord. He pulls it. A naked bulb bathes the cellar in light.

Reece and Evie shield their eyes. "Connor!" they both call.

"Don't worry." He fiddles with the ladder's housing and quickly snares the lever that will trigger the sliding mechanism. "You'll be out in a sec."

Moments later, all three children are sat on the hallway floor.

"So Bea's dead?" Reece asks, his eyes moist.

"I think so." Connor sighs.

"She seemed t' be Gary's favourite, though. After he'd knocked you out, he locked us two in the basement, but he let Bea stay with 'im."

"Doesn't make sense, does it?"

"We only met this mornin'," says Evie. "But it feels like we're best friends."

"I know. I wonder what 'appened to Mo 'n' Emily. I guess they were lucky. Well, we were lucky too, 'cause Gary didn't actually kill us —" A noise from the front door shuts his mouth.

"What's that?" Evie springs to her feet.

That is a tapping on the window, the kind a parent does before opening the door without waiting for an invitation.

The kids fly up the stairs and determine which room will grant the best view of the street out front. Fortunately, it's not the suite with the corpse guest, nor is it the locked one from which Connor fled. They pile into the room to the left of Connor's cell and roll up the blinds.

"Shit." The eldest youngster gulps at the sight of so many zombies. "Why so many of 'em? Why 'ere?"

Chapter 19 — Lena Adderley — 21:15

She all but falls from the final fence. Exhausted and frantic, Lena's had a testing couple of hours. The wall that divided Langworthy Chemicals – the building after DDN's, which was where she killed a zombie with a hammer – from Lightning Mail had proved insurmountable. It was smooth-sided, high and topped with jagged chunks of glass cemented into the surface. She searched for a way of breaking into the chemical plant in order to find a way up to its roof, which would hopefully give her a path to Lightning Mail, but to no avail.

Therefore, she was forced to climb back into DDN's. Creeping through its vast compound should've been a cinch, but there were at least three more undead monsters lurking in the gloom. They were easy enough to dodge; she decided not to engage them in battle. Doing so, however, wasted time she didn't have. As did the journey she took through the industrial park's roads. There were fewer zombies at large than earlier, a development that confused Lena, yet they were still sufficient in number to force her to favour stealth over speed.

Then, as if time wasn't already a dwindling commodity, she was forced to break into another factory one hundred yards from Evolve HQ. Upon turning onto Grainger Road, she found the approach to her destination was far too congested with crazed, reeking brain-munchers to take the direct route. So again, Lena resorted to scaling fences.

The final leg of her journey involved infiltrating her family business headquarters. It should've been the hardest step thus far. Newer than any of its neighbouring complexes, its security is as hi-tech as its questionable government links require. On this occasion, the zombies had done her a favour, however. A pile of dead bodies at the foot of one of Evolve's perimeter walls supplied a passable, though nausea-inducing, ramp. The electro-wire at the summit, installed following threats from eco-terrorists due to the company's experimentation with agricultural manipulation technology, was tangled and decorated with chunks of singed human skin. But there was a gap. One big enough for Lena to fit through.

And now she's in.

With less than three hours to prevent the destruction of her hometown.

Whether she's successful or not, the Adderley name is probably dead. She know she needs to make peace with her failure and concentrate on saving lives, but she's terrified by her father's potential reaction. It could kill him.

Which might be for the best now.

"Focus, Lena, for heaven's sake." Taking cover behind a row of barrels, she wills her heart-rate to slow. She imagines classical music in her head and practises the breathing exercises learnt years ago.

She's at ground zero now: Evolve head office. It's infested by rabid cannibals. She can hear them trying to breach the main factory building; she can smell their rancid, dying bodies. Apart from when she was chased into St Paul the Apostle's, she's never been in more danger.

So she needs to focus. *Breathe in, breathe out. Feel the drizzle on your face, the breeze in your damp hair. Smell the oil, the chemicals, even the zombies. Fix the moon in your gaze; ignore the stars twinkling amidst the clouds. Take it all in. Immerse yourself in your senses.*

Then she blocks them all out, and concentrates on what needs to be done.

First of all, her inhaler. She takes a dose, then replaces the device in her pocket.

Eyes flitting from one object to the next, she assesses the yard. There are places she can hide, doors and windows to investigate. She dashes from the barrels to a shipping container. Stands with her back to the corrugated iron and takes a peek around the corner. Now she has eyes on the closest security door, which leads to the Research and Development wing.

There's a black-clad, gas-masked figure sprawled across the threshold. Beneath him is a gun of some sort, larger than a handgun but smaller than a rifle, and a pool of dark liquid. *We don't have armed guards. Hell,* no one *has armed guards. Terrorism activity and heightened security or not. This is Britain!*

Is it the government, then?

For a moment, she feels nauseous. *Perhaps Captain Lunt anticipated my next move, headed here, and he's met a sticky end…*

No, there's a light on the wall, so she has a good view of the dead man. He's short and slender, not tall and hulking like Lunt. *So who is it? Have Harry and Anderson already been eliminated, and this is Villeneuve's next play? The villain hasn't been in touch for hours. If I come across any of these shady-looking characters, will they help me or shoot me?*

She doesn't have time for speculation. Head down, she bolts across the tarmac. She kneels beside the fallen soldier, knocking spent bullet cartridges away with her foot in the process. Gingerly, she gives him a poke. He doesn't react, so, taking care not to get blood on her hands, and keeping her eyes averted from the ruin of the gunman's throat, jaw and shoulder, she pulls the weapon from under his corpse. It's a submachine gun, the type armed police officers tend to use. She's never held a firearm before, let alone discharged one, but how hard can it be?

Probably harder than you think, and you won't find out till it's too late.

Lena feels better with the SMG strapped to her back. She has a plan, and she needs to follow said plan to its conclusion. Unless she does actually manage to find Dr Sofia Aslam, in which case, she may have to be flexible. Of course, Aslam is probably dead, but proceeding without at least attempting to consult with the professor would be an error. One that could cost lives, and not just Aslam's.

If anyone refused to evacuate when the outbreak was reported, it would be Sofia. Contrary by nature, and fiercely protective of her work, Evolve's chief scientist would fight tooth and nail to do what she thinks is right. Even if that means doing battle with the undead.

The entrance closest to the savaged man in black has a circular, frosted window at head height. Through the glass,

Lena sees tables and filing cabinets stacked up against the door. *Someone is still here, obviously. Someone not undead.* Using her pass card, and a spot of saliva on her finger for the DNA sensor, the company director triggers the lock. There's a click, and she pushes. The pile of debris won't move.

"Shit." She checks her watch. If she doesn't find the scientist by ten PM, she'll need to press on with Plan A.

Lena skirts the wall, heading left. She reaches the southwest point of the R&D wing and pops her around the corner for the briefest of moments. There are no zombies, no armed humans, so onwards she goes. Another fire exit is up ahead. Seeing this one cheers the exec's heart, for its door is hanging ajar, but her smile quickly fades. Blood-reddened glass glitters in the harsh glare of a spotlight on the perimeter fence.

Someone is here, but zombies have broken in, too.

Lena takes a final glance over her shoulder to ensure she's not being followed, steps around the scarlet-coated crystals and enters R&D. It's silent inside. If the undead have made entry at this point, they're either not being resisted, or they've been killed. Hopefully it's the latter.

Scouring her memory, Lena struggles to recall the last time she visited Aslam at her office. Their other three meetings were held on Adderley turf, in the Corporate wing. Not that it made any difference, for the scientist was pugnacious and obstinate irrespective of the battlefield selected.

She almost misses a left turn. The next right she remembers; now she's in the corridor which houses the research team's residential quarters.

Somewhere within R&D somebody fires a gun, and a man yells something incoherent.

Heavy, rapid, clumsy footsteps fall close by. *Oh, fuck.*

Lena pulls the carbine off her back and examines it in the stark red emergency light. She's watched action movies before, seen the characters cocking, loading and shooting. But the ugly piece of metal in her hands may as well be alien technology for all the sense it makes to her.

A screech of shoes up ahead jerks her head up like a leash on a dog. A male zombie in the uniform of a paramedic is twenty yards away. Briefly it looks at Lena as though about to address her. Then it lurches forwards.

Oh, fuck. I'm screwed.

She looks at the monster, at the SMG, back at the monster. Her bladder constricts. Her heart jackhammers. Her vision swims.

Have to use the gun like a club. Unless…

There were empty ammunition jackets next to the gun's previous keeper, so he must've been firing. Which means the weapon is probably ready to use.

The undead beast is within six feet, arms reaching for its supper, when Lena points and pulls the trigger. The noise is deafening. Even from such short range, several rounds go wide to ricochet off corridor walls, but two of the slugs fly true. One hits the zombie in its solar plexus; number two catches it in the mouth. The thing's skull snaps back like it's been punched. Blood sprays as metal cartridges bounce on the floor.

The zombie slumps to the ground, its gruesome head millimetres from Lena's foot. She prods it with her toe, and it doesn't respond.

Ears ringing, hands throbbing from the machine gun's recoil, Lena backs away. She closes her eyes, takes a few deep breaths and turns her back on the creature she's just slain.

When she looks up again, she sees a door bearing a 'DR ASLAM' plaque.

What if the doctor's already dead? What if she's not been taking her meds and has turned into one of them?

Another scream in the vicinity urges her onward. She raps the door, waits a moment, then knocks again.

"Who is it?" a female calls.

"It's Lena… we need to talk."

"Lena?"

"Yes, Lena Adderley. Your boss, for Christsake!"

"Adderley? What in the world are *you* doing here?"

"Just stop shouting, and let me in."

"Are you alone?"

"Yes."

The portal opens with a sci-fi swish. Standing arms folded, her unruly hair pulled into a ponytail, Dr Aslam looks even scattier than usual. "Come in."

"Thanks." Lena's glad to hear the door hiss closed. As she takes the chair offered, barely registering the diagrams and formulae scrawled on the white board by the scientist's desk, she feels her limbs turning to jelly. She's tired, stressed beyond comprehension, but she can't relax yet. Noting Aslam's trademark eyebrow-raised expression, she says, "Before you say it, I know. You told me so."

The slightest of smirks flickers across the other woman's face. "But I would never have predicted… this. Nor is it the time to gloat."

Gunfire carries through the walls again, making both jump.

"We obviously don't have much time. I don't know what your plans are —"

"— To stay put. I'm as safe behind my door as I would be anywhere else —"

"— Except you're not." Without revealing her source, Lena tells of Mortborough's impending doom.

"That won't contain the threat, Lena. I know you're not scientifically-minded, so I won't go into the details, but Resurrex can't simply be burnt out of existence. It's designed to react to heat, as plants do naturally with light. It'll just make things worse."

"Just another reason why we've got to stop the attack, then." Adderley explains her solution.

Aslam rolls her eyes. "Are you even listening to me?"

"What? Why?"

"Burning down this plant might save the Government. But Resurrex can't be destroyed by fire. In fact, its effects will be *accelerated* if you set this place ablaze."

"Can't we shut everything down safely?"

"The Resurrex in storage can be contaminated with other agents to render it safe —"

"— Great, so let's —"

"— But not by midnight. It's not a quick fix. And in any case, it won't solve the problem. It won't neutralise the Resurrex that's already been released. The wind is spreading the chemicals that've been sprayed, *and* the concentrated batch that was compromised in the lorry crash. It's a perfect storm, if you'll pardon the pun."

Lena massages her own temples. "So… that's it? We can't get rid of evidence of Evolve's links with the Government, so the strike goes ahead. Mortborough is destroyed. Any survivors are annihilated. But the Resurrex, which will be *more* reactive 'cause of the missiles, will keep spreading across the northwest. To places where they don't have the inhalers. There's no way of stopping it, so there will be more zombies. More missile strikes. And there's nothing we can do?"

Aslam exhales loudly through her nose. "Apart from praying for the wind to stop. And even then, the chemicals will disperse and proliferate. It's what they're designed to do."

"We're fucked. The whole country is fucked, essentially."

"Essentially."

Miraculously, the fall broke no bones. But if he'd known he was going to waste thirty minutes trying to get down off the roof safely, only to plummet into a dying shrub anyway, he would've simply thrown himself off to begin with.

For a moment, sat on the wet soil, the soldier's heart is in his mouth. He landed on the sat-phone in his pocket. If it's damaged, Brad's work on the roof will be in vain. The device seems fine, though. Now that Lunt's outside, the young IT geek's technological wizardry bears fruit: the phone has a signal. Somehow, before he came down through the skylight to help his friends, Brad did as requested and adapted the satellite dish to enable telecom services.

Lunt's first call is to Villeneuve, who starts by telling his employee to report to Ms Adderley. The politician ends the conversation with a stern warning: 'act first, ask questions later; eliminate any survivors you find, particularly anyone who might talk'. The fact the Right Honourable Gentleman was willing to speak so openly, without using code-words, about slaughtering civilians sends shivers down the Scotsman's spine.

The prospect of the second call fills Lunt with a mixture of dread and excitement. His sausage-like forefinger, still sore from prizing the cable ties from his wrists, trembles as he keys in Lena's number. He's scared she won't answer, anxious that she *can't* answer. Drizzle he barely feels sprinkles the phone's screen; he has to press the 'call' button twice.

After a moment, the dialling tone begins. He stands, wincing as he puts weight on his mangled foot. He dusts himself off with one hand while holding the cell-phone with the other. Glancing around, he detects no threat. It's dark, but the moon is bright, so visibility is good. He can't stay in one place for too long, however.

Ten agonising seconds later, the call connects.

"Hello?" Lena sounds like she's underwater. "Harry?"

"Lena." He clears his throat. "Where are ye?"

"Evolve HQ."

"Listen, I'm sorry I've been incommuni—"

"— Forget that, Harry. I need your help. Quick."

"Go on."

Lunt listens as she explains Operation Peterloo and describes the situation in the industrial estate. His mind is whirring. The aches and pains incurred over the last couple of hours are forgotten. "Midnight?"

"Yes, midnight. Fucking midnight." Her voice is brittle. This is her town, and it's about to be wiped off the map because of her company's mistakes. "The doctor and I have been racking our brains, but we're none the wiser. What can we do?"

"I'm no' sure. I'll think of somethin' on the way." He signs off.

Just fuckin' run, ye daft bastard. Don't risk yer life fer a woman you've barely spoken to fer years. Ye've got a wife at home, waitin' for ye. Fuck the job. This mission went tits-up the minute ye walked intae that beauty salon 'n' the owner came at ye. Shoulda got outta Dodge right there 'n' then.

Heedless of his better judgment, his legs are already moving. As he limps away from the castle, he ponders the stupidity of his actions. He has one pistol, the silenced Glock, which Brad talked the others into leaving for him. One clip. Plus the inhaler, of course, which he realises he's not used for a couple of hours; he takes a couple of tokes to compensate

Now he's heading to zombie central, if Lena's description is accurate. Death almost certainly awaits. Meaning his wife will be a widow for the last few months of her life. Which will be short, because there will be no pension or life insurance payment for her due to the clandestine nature of Lunt's agreement with Gordon Villeneuve. No way of paying for the private oncologist that was promised.

And why? her husband asks himself as he nears the park exit. Why is he digging his own grave?

'Cause a young, posh lassie, born wi' a whole drawer of silver cutlery in her mouth, never mind just a silver spoon, once gave ye a coupla months o' bloody romance. Coupla months o' the passion he's never truly felt for Maggie, as good a wife as she is. Shaggin' till they were too exhausted 'n' sore tae continue. Lyin' in each other's arms fer hours in the beds of various hotels across continental Europe.

He would prefer to claim altruistic motives – saving what's left of Mortborough's townsfolk – but he learnt not to lie to himself a long time ago. Lunt's braving the rise of the dead entirely because he's too sentimental to let Lena Adderley go.

The dead yellow grass by the way out is churned to mud. It'll never grow back now. Hundreds, maybe thousands of zombies came this way at some point, but they're gone. Like Lunt, they're headed for Evolve, their motives as nonsensical as his own.

On the edge of the park there lies a housing estate. Although cutting through a populated area will likely take him closer to danger, it'll save time. So he hurries onward, splashing through puddles, squinting against flurries of rain, gritting his teeth through the pain in his right foot. At first he takes the most direct route, via Ascot Street. Within fifty yards, however, he encounters the first hostile, a ragged-clothed, bloody-frocked, middle-aged woman standing beneath a street light.

He executes the zombie before it even realises he's there, blowing its brains against the lamppost, but there's another two further down the road. Reluctant to expend ammunition, he leaves the main road and uses sidestreets and alleyways.

As opiates drain from his system, he begins to feel the effects of the day's trials. The foot injury inflicted by Jada is a fireball of agony. Brad's mallet left an egg-sized lump on Lunt's skull that throbs incessantly. Luke, a fierce brawler with hands like stone, landed a few heavy blows. But they left him a shot of morphine and a gun, when many would've abandoned him to suffer then die unarmed.

Good kids, they were. Good kids ah tried tae shaft 'cause o' Lena fuckin' Adderley 'n' Gordon fuckin' Villeneuve.

The ex-serviceman emerges from yet another ginnel. He checks his phone; its signal is weakening. Lunt's at one end of a crescent now, a cul-de-sac, and he's worried he's taken a wrong turn. About to turn back, he hears something that stops him short. The undead vocalise sometimes, but that's not what he heard. They wheeze and splutter like old men who've smoked forty a day since they were teenagers. This was a growl.

Someone cries out, but the noise is swiftly muffled. Again the snarling, this time louder, more strident.

Drawing his pistol, Lunt scans the darkened houses of Cotton Crescent. Many have smashed windows; more have battered front doors. Only three vehicles are parked: one is on a driveway, another in the middle of the road, blackened by fire. The third, the closest to him, is parked roadside. An immobile mass is in the driver's seat.

Ignoring the pain in his foot, the former soldier stands and watches the occupied hatchback, which is only fifteen yards away. The merest of shadows shifts. A lamp-lit puddle under the Peugeot 309 darkens for a heartbeat. Then there's another sound, one which reminds Lunt of home.

Paws on the ground.

Claws scratching, worrying at something metal.

The big Scot flicks the Glock's safety switch, keeping the barrel pointing down. He takes a step forward.

The scrabbling stops, to be replaced by another growl, then moving feet.

It's a big dog, easily twelve stone, a mastiff. Its fawn fur is mottled with dark stains, its muzzle a riot of fangs, drool and blood. There's no fear in the eyes, only hunger. With a final grizzle, the predator lopes towards Lunt.

The ex-squaddie's always been quick on the draw, but he's never before fought a wild, fearless animal. By the time he's brought his handgun to bear, the creature has closed the distance and is leaping through the air. One of its forepaws strikes his arm, spoiling his aim. His shot misses; a car alarm blares; the pistol is sent flying. One hundred and seventy pounds of undead canine piles into Lunt's chest.

As he goes down, instincts take over. He catches the dog's throat with his right hand while grabbing the scruff of its neck with his left. The beast is strong. Even holding it in a two-handed grip, Lunt feels it overpowering him, like he's having an arm-wrestle with someone slightly more powerful. The mastiff's jaws gnash violently, as if it's already feasting, though its snub, ragged mouth is still six inches from the man's face.

Six inches but getting closer. Saliva and foamy blood shower onto Lunt's face. Sour breath assails his nostrils

Need tae get a better hold.

His fingers find a collar, which he grips. Turning his left wrist, he twists the choker, tightening it, forcing a thicker globule of spittle onto his cheek as the fang-filled mouth closes. The dog weakens, almost imperceptibly, but it's enough. Lunt seizes the lower mandible. With a vicious wrench, his left hand pulling towards him, his right pushing away, he breaks the mutt's neck.

Dead weight slumps across the exhausted victor. *Fuck me, that was close.* He lets the back of his head rest against the pavement for a moment, then shunts the carcass aside. Lunt suddenly realises he has potentially-infected slobber all over his skin. Cringing, he mops his face clean with the sleeve of his shirt.

The car on the driveway is still beeping, its lights flashing. He needs to get away before it attracts any more undead, especially now that animals are starting to turn.

After retrieving his pistol, Lunt turns to leave the crescent for the second time. Then he remembers the person in the 309, and Villeneuve's grisly orders echo through his mind.

Fuck it. I'll just pretend ah didnae see 'em.

A car door opens; Lunt huffs. *For Christsake. Now ah have nae choice.*

Gravel crunches beneath feet. "Hello?" a woman calls.

He doesn't want to turn around, for when he does, he'll see her face, and she'll see his. A contract of sorts will be exchanged. Two survivors, with a dead dog on the ground between them, their experiences of that day will be different but similar.

"Hello, mate?"

Lunt looks over his shoulder. She's average height, a little plump, with chestnut-coloured skin. Her white dress is daubed with blood, which looks like oil under the stark streetlight. As if by telepathy, she seems reluctant to approach her saviour.

"Y'alright, hen?"

"Ah, yeah. Who are you?"

"Name's Harry." *Why did you tell her yer name, dimwit? Now ye'll have tae kill her.* "What's yer name?" *What the fuck, man? Why would ye wannae know her name? Now killin' her will be even harder.*

"Ashara. Ashara Ndlovu."

The car alarm has stopped. Apart from the wind and rain, silence reigns.

"Come on, we better get goin'." The Scotsman sheaths his pistol and heads back down the ginnel. *I'll kill her. I'm no' soft. But I'll do it somewhere more remote. Someone could be lookin' outta the window 'round here.*

"So why the gun?" she pants, her shorter legs working harder to keep up.

Lunt exits the alleyway after checking both ways: Baker Drive is clear. "Comes in useful."

"I'm sure it does, 'Arry. But why do you 'ave it in the first place?"

"Never ye mind. Let's get a move on."

"Where we goin', like?"

"Somewhere else."

"Yer very mysterious, 'Arry. Are you part o' some sorta cover-up? I saw a movie once, with zombies, 'n' the Army came 'n' started quarantinin' everyone, 'n' some tried to escape, 'n' —"

"— Just…" Lunt stops abruptly, sending a white-hot knife of pain through his foot. *Ye should shoot her now, Harry.* "Just be quiet a minute, hen. Ah need tae think."

Yer no' gonnae shoot her, are ye?

"Not that I've seen any army, like." Ashara's tone is nonchalant, as though the apocalypse is an everyday occurrence. "All I've seen is them 'orrible zombie fuckers. Lucky I was at 'ome, like. Bet m' mum 'n' dad are both dead now, though."

"Ye don't know that fer definite, lassie." He points down a street. "This way."

"'Ang on. I must know these ends better than you. What wi' you bein' Scotch, 'n' that. So why don't you tell *me* where we're goin', 'n' I'll lead the way?"

Lunt blows a long breath through pursed lips. "Okay. You win. Ah need tae get tae the industrial estate. Ye know the big one, near the church?"

"Oh yeah." She strides ahead. "I used t' work in a ware'ouse there. Shit job, paid peanuts. Follow me, 'Arry."

He reaches for his hip, unfastens the holster and begins to ease the Glock free. *Just get it over wi', Harry, fer fucksake. Back o' the head, she won't feel a thing.*

Chapter 21 — Connor Norman — 22:05

Inexplicably, he enjoys the responsibility of caring for the younger kids. Of course, he wishes the circumstances were different; he would prefer to be babysitting because their parents had gone to the pub, rather than because their parents had been eaten.

Maybe my *mum 'n' dad aren't dead, though. They* might *still be alive.*

Yeah, right.

He takes a puff on his inhaler and looks pointedly at Reece and Evie, who are sat on the bed. "'Ave you been usin' yer inhalers?"

Evie nods with enthusiasm, but Reece looks at his lap.

"What?" Connor stands. The banging on the door and the rattling of the window bars are forgotten. "Take it, now!"

"I… I lost it." Tears well in the smaller boy's eyes. "Sorry."

Go easy on 'im. 'He's only little. He sits back down on the camping chair taken from the kitchen. "When, Reece?"

"This mornin'."

Connor bites his lip. "'Ave some o' mine, then." He hands over his medicine, and Reece obeys, while Evie takes a hit on her own. Everyone is quiet for a moment.

"'Ow long d' ya think it'll take?" Evie keeps glancing at the Venetian blinds. The first floor windows aren't protected by iron, but, so far, none of the hundred or so zombies have attempted to make the climb. "For 'em to get in, I mean."

"Dunno." Connor doesn't like this part about leading the Mortborough Monster Murderers, as the trio have dubbed themselves. His lieutenants expect him to have the answers to everything, even though he's in exactly the same situation as them. *No, 'dunno' isn't good enough. I need t' reassure them, keep 'em calm.* "The bars look pretty strong. 'Opefully, they'll get bored soon. We just need t' be quiet. I reckon they came 'ere 'cause of all the noise Gary was makin'."

"'N what if Gary comes back?" Reece wonders.

"He'll see all the zombies, 'n' he'll go try 'n' find some other kids to molest." *Shit, I shouldn't have said that.* "Gary didn't, ya know, do anythin' t' you two, did he? When he 'ad ya locked up, I mean."

Both children shake their heads convincingly.

Thank god fer that.

Just chill out, Connor. Be careful what ya say, but chill. He takes a deep breath through his nostrils, the way Mum does when she gets a message from Dad. It's musty in Room 4, probably due to the black damp stains scattered across the walls and ceiling. Even with the window open – smashed by Connor earlier when he was escaping Room 2 – the smell lingers. But at least it doesn't reek as badly as Room 3, where the old lady is rotting.

"Do ya think we should be called 'Murderers'?" Reece wonders. "I mean, we've not actually murdered any zombies, 'ave we? Just run away from 'em, like."

Connor watches the smaller boy as he speaks: Reece's going paler, and his nose is starting to run. "We've not murdered any *yet*. We will if they try 'n' get in 'ere, though, won't we?" His bravado is forced, but it seems to impress the kids.

Reece is definitely gettin' ill, which is probably because he's turnin' into a zombie, 'n' when he really does turn, me 'n' Evie'll be screwed. Maybe we should lock 'im in the basement again, just to be sure —

Another window smashes. The latest to be compromised is not on the ground floor, however, which means the MMMs are in trouble.

"Stay 'ere." Connor leaps to his feet. Ignoring Reece and Evie's protests, he reaches for his trusty lamp and leaves the room. Obviously, he's scared, but he feels less terrified simply by pretending to be brave.

Straight away, he knows where to go. In order to reach the first floor, the enemy must've climbed onto the Victorian brick outhouse that stands next to the kitchen wall, which means they'll be coming in via Room 1. The door is locked, for every upstairs room has a lock on the outside, so the zombie will have to smash through. It's not wasting any time. Seconds after its feet hit the chamber's floorboards, it commences its assault on the door.

Does Connor wait for the zomb to force entry? Or should he open up, let the monster through, and then murder it? Option two is the most daunting. It means the door remains intact, though, which could buy the kids time if a large number of undead follows the first onto the outdoor toilet roof and in via the window.

His decision is rendered moot when, after the seventh blow, the lock breaks. Instead of turning the doorknob, the mindless beast continues to attack until a hole appears at adult head height. A face appears. The zombette was pretty once. Now its high cheekbones are gashed to the bone. The eyes are bloodshot, the perfect teeth red with someone else's insides, afro hair matted and uprooted in patches.

MMM leader Connor Norman hefts the lamp in both hands. *Just run! Get in one o' the other rooms, or go downstairs to the basement. Do anythin' other than fightin' this crazy bitch!* But these animals, or ones like them, probably killed Connor's mother, maybe even his father. They've rampaged across Mortborough unopposed, bashing, biting and ingesting those too slow or afraid or overwhelmed to defend themselves.

Nostrils flaring, the boy swings his rudimentary club. There's a sickening thud. The zombie sags for a heartbeat. Then it recovers and squeezes an arm through the ever-widening fissure in the door.

This time Connor grunts as he lashes out with every ounce of strength in his small body. Crimson sprays; bone crunches; the intruder is stopped for good.

He stands stock still for a moment. Blood drips from the base of the lamp to the floor. A thicker stream seeps from the zombie's head. It dribbles onto a brown-skinned forearm, circles the wrist and falls onto the ground.

I did it. I am *a Mortborough Monster Murderer. Fuck, yeah! But… but that means I am a murderer, period. I just killed someone, a cannibal psycho, yeah, but still a person. If a cure is found, this woman won't be 'ealed. She'll be buried.*

He shakes his head. She's not a 'she', she's an 'it'. The young man was given a choice. It or him, life or death, and it would've been devouring him by now had he not crumpled its skull into its brain.

Why are they doing it, though? Why are normal people, this one a nurse or carer judging by her blue tunic and sanitary gloves, dying and coming back as man-eating maniacs? The premise is as ridiculous and disturbing as the sight before him: a battered door with a gory head and arm sprouting from it. It's an unholy haunted-house-mutating-into-a-demon scenario that even the most unhinged of horror movie directors wouldn't imagine.

Connor sighs; he's wasting time and brainpower puzzling over the whys and wherefores. He gives Room 1's door a tentative push, but the dead freak's weight stops it opening. So he shoves harder, then recoils as the corpse dislodges and disappears from view. A few seconds pass before he opens the door, as he wants to make sure the zombie doesn't rise again.

"Evie, Reece?" he calls.

"Yeah?" they chorus.

"I'm good. Just don't… just stay in there fer now, yeah?"

Evie voices her assent, while Reece coughs.

After switching on Room 1's light, Connor steps around the twice-dead body. His pulse quickens again as he treads towards the gaping, jagged-edged window.

Dirty-nailed fingers appear on the window ledge. "Shit!" He pulls away.

Another set of digits emerge, two feet from the first. The second lot is crusty with blood, with the ring-finger severed.

Without thinking, the kid clears a couple of shards of glass, then uses the lamp as a hammer. He pulverises three fingers on one hand and two on the other before the invader relinquishes its grip. Connor looks down, out of the window, to see the dead old man land on the outhouse's roof with a crash.

Slates scatter; a gutter collapses, covering climbing undead with debris. Connor grins, because now the enemy have no way of reaching the window. Naturally, the thirty-odd moonlit zombies continue to try, scrambling over each other, slipping as rubble shifts under their feet.

He heads back to the other two MMMs to impart the good news.

"Awesome!" Evie says. "So we're safe fer now? Are they leavin'?"

"Not yet." Connor sets the 'Lampinator' on the floor and sits down. His hands are shaking, so he grips his knees. "It'll take 'em a while before they work out they can't get in."

"What if they climb up another 'ouse?" Reece croaks. He cuffs mucus from his nose, then coughs again. "Next door, maybe. They could use the walls 'n' drainpipes, like you did."

"I don't think they're that smart." Connor tries not to stare at the younger lad's weeping eyes and clammy brow. *Maybe it's just the lightin' in 'ere, too bright without a lampshade, and the lad's not as poorly as he looks. Perhaps if they just try 'n' forget about it, Reece'll be fine. The power of positive thinkin', as Mum says.* But he's the leader, so he can't shy away from difficult situations. "Are ya feelin' okay, Reece? You don't look well."

"I'm fine, honestly, just a little bit of a cold, that's —" This time the coughing fit is prolonged, only ending when a dark chunk of sputum is propelled from Reece's mouth onto the floor.

At first, Evie quails, but she swiftly recovers to put an arm around her stricken comrade.

Meanwhile, Connor has frozen. *Come on, dumb-ass, pull yerself together. Just a bit o' snot. Reece might 'ave the flu, or whatever. Can't panic now. I'm the leader.* He sits next to Reece on the bed. "You good, bro? Should we get you a glass o' water?"

After a moment, the other boy settles. His breathing is raspy, though, as if he has sandpaper in his throat. "I'm good." Reece accepts a pillowcase from Evie and uses it as a handkerchief. As soon as he's cleared his face of perspiration, fresh beads appear. "Water'd be cool, though." He splutters again, but only once.

Evie scampers away. Her footsteps on the stairs echo through the old building.

"Take some more o' this." Connor hits his inhaler first and hands it over. *I'll 'ave to wash it before I use it next.*

Reece smiles wanly and raises the device to his mouth, his fingers shivering so badly that the plastic rattles his teeth. He simultaneously depresses the button and sucks. Then he repeats the process. His second dose triggers another round of coughing, equally as violent as the one that produced the bloody discharge.

Except that this one doesn't end.

In fact, Reece is still barking away when Evie returns. His hands, covering his mouth, are misted scarlet. His narrow shoulders shudder. He's like a glitching robot, performing the same action over and again, always the same...

Until he stops. With one final wheeze, Reece falls into Connor, who starts, having been a passive observer for what feels like an hour by this point. The lifeless kid's final moments were almost an out-of-body experience for the leader of the MMMs.

The five minute silence that follows is almost a relief. No one moves; Reece's head rests on his friend's arm. Then Evie begins to weep, as does Connor, more quietly.

Time to get my shit together. Heavy-hearted, he settles Reece onto the bed. "Are you alright?" he asks Evie.

"Yeah." She swallows, still looking at the small, motionless body between them. "Well, no, not really. I only knew 'im a few hours, but it feels like weeks."

"At least the zombies seem to 'ave given up."

"Yeah. Thought they'd be bangin' away all night. Sometimes, you know what they're gonna do, but other times, they take ya by surprise. Proper messes with yer 'ead."

"Better they mess with our 'eads than munch on our 'eads."

"I guess. I just wanna go 'ome."

"I know." He pats her little white hand. "Me too." *Except there is no 'ome. Nothin' left except us 'n' these zombies.*

"I don't even know if m' mum 'n' dad are still alive, but I still just wanna…"

"What? You just wanna what?"

"He's movin'." Evie's become as rigid as the dead boy by her side. "Look."

She's right, and so was Connor when he feared Reece turning into one of *them*.

He is moving.

Chapter 22 — Jada Blakowska — 22:20

"Your story checks out." Gould stands in the bus station canteen doorway, all smiles. As if he's not just get them prisoner for the last couple of hours.

"Excellent," she replies with an acidic look. She snaps her miniature notepad shut and feeds her pen through the rings at the top. Her attachment to paper and ink has been laughed at in the past, but it's proving useful at the moment.

Luke shoots to his feet, upsetting his plastic chair. "Fuck are you talkin' about?" He's been winding himself up since Gould led them at gunpoint into the refectory. Being imprisoned for the second time that day enraged him, and the thought that his son could perish in the meantime added fuel to the flames.

"I'll explain shortly." Gould runs a hand through curly, damp, salt-and-pepper hair and straightens his public transport company tie. "The main thing is, my friend and I have authorised the commandeering of one of the buses. Intelligence we've sourced suggests now would be the optimal time to depart. So are you coming, or not?"

Luke's still seething. He's placated, though, by the promise of seeking out Connor.

Brad rises to his feet, slowly and deliberately. He now seems devoid of any emotion. During their stint as bus station jail inmates, he's slipped into a deep depression once more. Of course, it's been less than half a day since he killed his own undead daughter, so his two companions aren't surprised by his deterioration.

Jada stands and puts her notepad in her back pocket.

"What's that you've got there?" Gould asks as she approaches, his eyes slitted. He has a tendency to switch from affable to paranoid in a heartbeat.

"Just my notes." Following Luke and Brad, she passes Gould in the doorway.

"Notes?"

"Yeah."

"Okay… I'm just gonna come out and say it. Are you a *spy*?"

"No, I'm not a fuckin' spy. I'm a journalist. Which you should know, since you've supposedly 'checked out' our 'story'. She continues down the corridor towards the open external door, grateful for the fresh air. "God knows how you did that, by the way, given there's no working Internet anywhere, and Luke, Brad and I are hardly household names."

"I conferred with a friend!" Gould insists. "Plus I have other sources." He's at least six yards behind everyone else. Presumably still pointing his ludicrously large revolver at their backs.

"Yeah, right." Jada emerges into the cooler night air. The rain has stopped by this point, though the bus awaiting them is still wet. "So, your mysterious 'friend'. Is he gonna make an appearance at some point?"

Gould halts. "When he's ready. But you're changing the subject. What's in your notes?"

Stood by the single-decker, hands on hips, Luke's eyes burn. "Can we move it along a little, please? Ya can argue 'bout this while I'm driving."

Midway across the concourse, Jada hears the revolver being cocked. She feels a strong sense of déjà vu.

"The notepad," Gould growls. "Give it to me, now."

She sighs, turns and pulls the pad from her pocket. "How about a compromise, then? I know you have your gun, and our guns, but we could be useful to each other."

The middle-aged man lowers his handgun by a few degrees. He's sweating profusely and is dark under the eyes, but he's looked the same since he ambushed them earlier. "Go on. Make your point."

"If you tell us about your friend, *and* tell us why you supposedly know so much about what's goin' on here in Mortborough, I'll share, too."

"Fair enough. But like your friend said, we might as well do that on the bus. Then we can find Connor. We don't have much time, according to my sources."

"Finally! Someone's talkin' sense." Luke presses the bus door release button, lets Brad past and climbs aboard. "Hang on a sec. How d' you know my son's name?"

Gould, marching briskly to catch up, tuts. "How many times? I have *sources*."

Once they're all seated, Luke drives the bus onto the main road. Jada suggested Gould take the wheel, as he was once a bus driver, but he's clearly too suspicious to sit with his back to everyone else.

Judging by its pine and lavender scent, the bus has been recently cleaned. The sounds of a city in chaos are muted by the drone of the engine. Like Brad, Jada looks out of the window at the dark streets. At night the destruction is less obvious; she can almost pretend none of it has happened. But they've barely travelled a hundred yards before they reach a roadblock and are forced to turn around.

Gould clears his throat, startling her. "So. Your notebook?"

"You first. Your 'intelligence'?"

"I have a gun, remember. I call the shots, as it were."

"Touché. Okay." She fishes the book from her pocket. "It's too dark." Once Gould's turned on the lights, she continues. "It's nothing to get excited about. If I make it through this, I'm gonna write an article, probably a book. So I'm just recording thoughts about the —"

"— *Thoughts*? I'm not interested in 'thoughts'. I want facts!"

"Will theories do?"

"Maybe. Try me."

"The inhalers. I've seen —"

"— What about them?"

"I've seen you use yours. In fact, I'm probably overdue a hit on mine. I think we can safely say that they are making us immune to the zombies, and —"

"— Obviously —"

"— Let 'er finish, mate," Luke calls from the cabin.

"Certainly." Gould's scornful expression suddenly gives way to one of contrition. He sets the revolver down on the seat next to him. "Do continue, Jada."

She explains her hypothesis about Evolve's chemicals causing the outbreak.

"That would make sense. In fact, my associates have been keeping an eye on Evolve."

"Then they're very wise. Anyway, I'm not sure if you're aware, but several Evolve board members also have stakes in another company, Pharmaco. They produce and sell the inhalers."

Once again, they grind to a standstill. Cursing, Luke reverses in order to use a sidestreet as a turning point. As he stops on the narrower road, something hits one side of the vehicle.

Brad flinches. "One o' them. Just jumped into the window."

Then there's a bang behind Jada. She spins in her seat to see a shadowy figure launching itself into the bus again, cracking the glass. Others are close behind, too. "Go, Luke, go!"

The driver slams the gas, shunting them away from the horde. Impacts against the rear of the PCV are intense for a moment, but they quickly die away.

"The benefits of public transport," Brad says, dully.

Everyone else smiles in relief.

Gould rubs his stubbled jaw. "Anyway. Evolve and Pharmaco. They're making money both ways. It's cynical, but not illegal, and it kinda pales into insignificance compared to what we've witnessed today."

"Yeah, fair enough." Jada's gaze is now intent on the high street outside. They pass the occasional zombie, but they seem too bewildered to cause the group any trouble. "But I did a bit o' digging last week, so that when I interviewed Sofia Aslam, I'd have some dirt to scare her with. Of all the people that are involved in both Evolve and Pharmaco, only one is well known to the general public."

"Who?"

"Gordon Villeneuve."

"The MP? Works for DEFRA?"

"The very same."

"What's DEFRA?"

"Department for the Environment, Food and Rural Affairs," Luke says over his shoulder." "She reckons the Government'll try 'n' cover all o' this up."

They've slowed to take a corner, and a zombie rushes at the window by Gould. Deep in thought, he doesn't react. "They will if they think it'll come back and bite them on the arse. And you know what that'll look like?"

Jada's microbladed eyebrows raise. "What?"

"Black ops. Stealth strikes. Mercenaries storming in, guns blazing. Bad times, even worse than they are already."

"Like Lunt and Anderson," Brad states.

"Worse than them, Lunt said," Luke reminds the others.

Gould's lips flutter for a moment, and he nods to himself. "DEFRA have been under fire recently. They're expected to do something about the farming crisis, so they've obviously rushed into bed with Evolve." He accepts the journal passed to him by Jada and spends a minute flicking through its pages before returning it. "So what do you intend to do, anyway?"

"Expose the bastards. Make sure they pay for turning my town into… this." Jada's gripping her pen so tightly that her knuckles are blanching. "Right. Anyway. Your turn now, Gould. What do *you* know, and *how* do you know it?"

"Like your buddy Brad, I'm a bit of a tech-wiz. Working as the company's security manager, watching CCTV videos all day, is very dull. I learnt how to hack into feeds from other organisations, like the police, hospitals, et cetera. Therefore, I've had a pretty good idea what's been going on."

Another blockage: Luke swings the big steering wheel to the right. "That doesn't explain how ya know Connor's name. D' ya know what's happened to 'im? 'Cause if ya do, 'n' you've been holdin' out on us, there'll be trouble, gun or no gun."

"I know nothing about your son. I watched you guys talkin' for a few minutes on the canteen feed, when you were locked up. I used to have ear problems, so I'm a pretty good lip-reader."

Luke deflates. He thumps the steering wheel three times, hard.

Poor guy. I really hope we find Connor. Jada says a silent prayer, then turns to a fresh page in her notepad and eyeballs Josh Gould. "That all sounds a little far-fetched. But compared to some o' the things I've seen today, I guess it's pretty tame. Who's this 'friend', though, that you've mentioned?"

The man grins broadly and taps his temple. "He's in here."

"In *there*? What do you mean…"

"You'll probably say I'm mental. Hell, *I* used to think I was mental, but I've learnt to trust my friend."

"Okay." Jada bites her lip. "Hang on, Luke, why we slowin' down?"

Brad shrugs, as if she asked him.

"Wait a sec," Luke says, slowing to a walking pace. "Someone in the road… not a zombie… I'm sure that's… no, it can't be…"

"Who?"

"Geraint! It's Geraint, sits next t' me at work. Wondered where he'd disappeared to."

"Fuckin' weirdo, bro," Brad perks up suddenly. "Remember that woman who said she caught 'im in the stationery cupboard, messin' with 'imself —"

"Shit, he's in trouble." Luke points down the dual carriageway. A couple of dozen undead are gathered around a white van, but some are breaking away from the group to pursue Geraint, who's sprinting towards the bus.

Gould gets up and opens the doors, while Luke brakes. As soon as the fugitive jumps in, the driver accelerates, running down two of the zombies.

"Thank you, thank you *so* much," Geraint gushes. "My van broke down, and… and…" All of a sudden, the newcomer looks mortified. *Like he's escaped from zombies, only to rescued by vampires. Actually, that might make a good line in my new article slash book —*

"What's wrong, Geraint?" Luke asks.

"Take a seat. Rest." Gould smiles, but he's placed a hand on his gun.

"I… I didn't realise it was you, Luke. And… Brett, is it?"

"Brad." The younger man frowns. "What's goin' down, Geraint?"

"Nothing. I'm just surprised, that's all." The ginger-haired fellow glances at the passenger exit. "Nice to see friendly faces, with all of his horror."

"You were on your own, then?" Gould asks. "I'm Josh, by the way."

"No, I mean yes, I was on my own. I *am* on my own." Again his eyes flicker to his right. He's still standing.

Something's not right. He's been hunted by cannibals like the rest of us, but his behaviour isn't that of someone who's narrowly avoided death. It's furtive, almost shameful. Something is not right.

"Not far now." Luke has to all but stop the bus to take a sharp bend to the left. "Nearly at Connor's." His voice is tremulous, his tone a mixture of hope and dread.

When they pull up outside, Jada knows immediately that they'll find nothing; Gould voices the same conclusion under his breath. Luke and Brad jump out of the bus, fly through the gate, kick open the door, pile inside. A few minutes later, they re-emerge, and the taller man's dispirited face tells its own story. Walking back down the drive, Luke shakes his head.

Suddenly, Geraint jabs at a button on the ceiling. The doors open, and he alights, landing in a puddle, stumbling, then sprinting away from a perplexed Luke and Brad.

"What the fuck?" they say in synchrony.

"Go after him!" Jada is up and out of her seat before anyone else reacts. "Come on, before we lose him!"

Out of the still-open door she goes, onto the tarmac, with the others close behind.

Chapter 23 — Harry Lunt — 22:40

Six bullets remain in the Glock's clip. Cutting through the shopping precinct was an error, costly in terms of time and ammunition. Almost fatal, too, for the zombie infant that pounced from the flat's balcony had almost sunken its baby teeth into his neck. A ragged collar and a newfound fear of blonde preschool girls are Lunt's only scars.

Running from the mob took him away from rather than towards the industrial estate. If Lena's intel is sound, he has seventy minutes to help her prevent hellfire raining down on Mortborough. So finding the classic motorcycle, its bloodstained keys still in the ignition, on the road that leads to the closest motorway is a welcome surprise. He heaves it upright, switches on the ignition and climbs onto the seat.

Ah could just scoot outta here right now. Keep goin', never lookin' back, all the way home t' Maggie 'n' Bruce. We could be walkin' by the Loch tomorrow, chattin' 'bout nothin'.

Leaving Lena and any remaining Mortborians to die.

Not an option, buddy.

The motorbike's rumble hasn't gone unnoticed. Three zombies, a man, woman and child dressed as if they were on their way to the airport for a beach holiday, are leaving a corner shop and heading Lunt's way. The Scotsman rides, eyes squinting against the wind. His mode of transport will attract attention. But if he's to get to Evolve in time to save Lena and her town, he needs to be quick.

As he twists and turns, using pavements to dodge roadblocks and alleys as shortcuts, he realises he'll be reaching Lena empty-handed. He told her he would think of a way of stopping the Government's surgical strike. *Yer a fool, Harry. Tryin' tae be the hero, makin' promises ye cannae keep.* She's cleverer than him, so if she was unable to come up with a solution, he doesn't stand a chance.

Making good time, he turns onto Tintagel Road, which will take him almost all of the way to Highgrove Industrial. There are more abandoned cars in the town centre, more obstacles to swerve. Undead folk, gathered around corpses gnawed to the bone, reach out as he passes. A couple of dead dogs give chase. The only one to cause concern is a whippet that almost catches him when he slows to dodge a burnt-out bus. The fleet-footed canine gets a mouthful of Lunt's trouser leg for its trouble, but no flesh or blood.

As he spots St Paul's church in the distance, he comes to a conclusion. There's no safe way of eradicating the link between Resurrex and Her Majesty's Government. The missile attack is inevitable. All he can do is get Lena and Dr Aslam to safety. Jada, Brad, Luke – plus the latter's son, if he's not already dead – will die, unless they've already left the area. Hundreds more will perish. As will thousands of undead.

One day, scientists will figure out the truth behind the outbreak, and a cure for the plague will be developed. It will be too late for the residents of Mortborough, who will be obliterated with the click of a button. Of course, the bombing won't kill *everyone*. Drones will mop up afterwards, while rank-and-file soldiers impose martial law on the surrounding areas. Specialist units will be utilised to silence the media.

Meanwhile, the likes o' Villeneuve'll come out smellin' o' roses. Fuckin' bastards. No one'll ever know the part they played startin' this shit-storm.

He should be angry with Lena as well. Her company's chemicals have caused havoc on a biblical scale. Knowing her, she won't have deliberately put lives in danger, but she's headstrong, and she would take risks and cut corners if she felt it necessary. Deep down, though, she has a good heart. *Or am ah just believin' what ah wannae believe?*

Regardless, that recklessness of hers has led to *this*.

Lunt applies the brakes fifty yards short of St Paul's, his eyes fixated on perhaps the most disquieting sight he's witnessed thus far. With the moon fat above them, shadowy zombies are digging in the cemetery, scrabbling through soil and clay to find rotting bones on which to feed.

Jesus wept. They must be fuckin' hungry, 'n' there can't be much in the way o' prey around if they're resortin' to dry auld skeletons.

He has a choice. Apart from those haunting the graveyard, there are roughly one hundred undead milling around the junction of Armitage Road and Grainger Road. Finding another way into Highgrove will be less hazardous, but it will take too long. So Lunt allows the bike to roll as far it will go without acceleration, praying none of the hostiles hear the wheels.

Once he's within twenty yards, the closest register his approach. He revs the throttle and aims the handlebars for the broadest gap between bodies. The tyres screech on the damp road surface for a split second; then he's hurtling towards the horde. The noise wakes the idle zombies from their trance. Jostling one another, they surge towards the motorcyclist. Most do so mindlessly, failing to adjust their advance as the bike moves, arriving too late, colliding with their brethren.

Some are cannier, though. Just as Lunt is about to turn onto Grainger, a group of zombies block the way. A horizontally-parked car across the pavement to his left means he must pull hard to the right. Not too hard, though, because there's a van on the opposite side. He over-corrects, at too high a speed. Heart in mouth, he strives to maintain control. But the back wheel's lost traction. He leaps clear as the motorcycle goes into a slide. While rolling, he hears a smash as the bike slams into something. The pain is forgotten as soon as he stops tumbling. Scenting blood, the enemy are closing in.

Lunt knocks the nearest off its feet with a kick to the shin. Grabs an ankle and yanks. A female zombie goes down; its skull hits the kerb with a gratifying crack. Going for his pistol now. Suddenly the moon disappears as a mass descends. He just about angles his Glock up in time to blast the pouncing zombie, which lands on the survivor's midriff, lifeless.

Squirming clear, he headshots another before it gets too close. *Need to get up.* He sits, then has to twist at the waist when a boy zombie rushes him. The little beast takes a .45 round between the eyes.

On yer feet, soldier.

As the Scotsman stands, a meaty hand grabs his shoulder. He spins and pistol whips the former construction worker just as its red-lipped mouth opens. Teeth shatter.

Lunt pushes the stunned fiend into one behind it. Both trip over a crawling, dead paraplegic.

Tearing away from something grabbing his leg, the former squaddie sees a way clear. He sprints, weaving between grasping hands until the majority of undead are in his wake.

Every sense is heightened: a smell of smoke competes with that of putrefying bodies; the coolness of the night breeze; rattles and snickers of zombies in the vicinity.

The arch that demarks the entry to Highgrove Industrial Estate is just feet away. If he can just reach it… he'll still have another half a mile to travel. He's beginning to tire, but every hostile he passes will be fresh, full of bloodlust.

Yer fucked, Harry, ye daft wee cunt. Ye've only three shots left. Ye'll be some ugly bastard's dinner soon enough.

The big man reaches an intersection, sees signs for Evolve plc, carries on running. He passes a meat processing plant, realising too late that, behind its half open shutters, there are dozens of zombies. They must prefer live, warm flesh to frozen, because they stream out of the building to dog his footsteps.

"Fuck." Lunt's lungs feel ready to implode. Every injury incurred today aches. Vertigo threatens to undermine him.

Then, passing a sidestreet to his right, he sees a black van. Its driver-side door yawns an invitation, so he bears that way. The dead are coming from up ahead, as if they're racing him to the vehicle. But if he can just climb in, shut the doors…

He skids to a stop beside the van. A black-cladded, helmeted soldier is seated, slumped over the steering wheel.

Footsteps are approaching.

The man in black's holster is empty. Lunt's eyes flicker from one side of the cabin to the other: there it is, a glint of black metal.

Gasping, wheezing, just yards away.

The Scotsman reaches over the dead man and under the passenger seat to grab the pistol. Without standing, he turns at the hip and blasts an obese zombie. One to the chest, then one through its hard hat as it lurches for him.

When the fat zomb goes down, a second, a power-suited woman, trips over the corpse.

Lunt shoots its ginger head then headshots two more emerging from behind the van.

"Fuck." They're all dead. No doubt more will be along soon, though, so Lunt tucks the Glock 19 in his waistband and opens the vehicle's side cargo door.

Like Christmas come early. Must be special forces o' some sort.

He pilfers a Sig Sauer MCX carbine, a Remington 870 pump-action, ammunition for both, plus sufficient grenades and explosives to take out a small army. After stowing the latter in a duffel bag that he straps to his back, the newly-rearmed soldier reaches to his pocket for the sat-phone. It's gone, presumably lost during the brawl near the church.

Muttering a curse, he continues towards his goal. The moon is bright, the blood black when it sprays from any undead that cross Lunt's path while jogging towards his destination. *This is more like it. Shit loads of ammo, deadly weapons, plentiful targets.* He doesn't usually enjoy his work these days. There's too much of an emphasis on stealth, too many civilians involved. Right now, however, he's in his element.

As he leaves dead heads pierced with high velocity rounds or shotgunned to oblivion, a small part of him recognises that he is, in fact, doing exactly what he was reluctant to do when he arrived in Mortborough that morning. He's engaging unarmed individuals who made no conscious decision to join battle.

But, he supposes, sniping a zombie climbing out of a dumpster, he has no choice. It's them or him. The only way he could avoid slaughtering innocents – like the diminutive female he shoots in the throat when it darts from behind an overturned ambulance a hundred yards from Evolve's front gates, or the teenaged girl he almost decapitates with a 12 gauge shell at close range as it jumps out from the security guard cabin – would be to walk away. Quitting now, though, will only cause more deaths. Even if he can only help Lena and Aslam, that'll be better than nothing.

Stay or go, he'll have blood on his hands, but he would sooner it be that of the undead than the living. He's stuck to his newfound principles as best as he can. Although doing so may affect his career prospects, he doesn't care. With Anderson dead, the escape of Luke, Jada and Brad ought to remain a secret. Ashara Ndlovu, the girl he couldn't bring himself to liquidate, even from behind, may be a different matter. He tried his best to scare her into silence; she might die soon in any case. But if she survives, and shares her story, Lunt could come to regret the loss of the killer instinct that has served him well in the past.

The retired captain takes a moment to catch his breath at the guard post. The compound's reinforced entry gates yawn wide, and the chemical plant's car park is fifty yards away. Well over a thousand undead are present. Some are attempting to break into the corporate section at the front of the complex; others are heading to either side to flank the office building. Most simply blunder around, drifting between vans and lorries. They've travelled across town, and now they're here, they seem aimless. Perhaps they're disappointed. Or more likely hungry.

Lunt tries to plot a route between the pockets of zombies. They're in such numbers, though, that he suspects he may have to advance from a different angle.

Hang on a minute.

Atop the corporate building, there are two silhouettes. Both have long, dark hair; both wear dark clothes. Lunt is annoyed by the way his heart soars as he realises Lena is still alive.

Is that a gun she's holdin'? Lena Adderley wi' a gun?

Armed or not, she's not getting down from the roof without help. Due to its smooth marble finish, the front wall of Evolve's office suite is impossible for the zombies to climb, but equally, there's no way for her and Aslam to descend. And even if they could, they would be landing in a world of teeth and madness.

"Right," Lunt murmurs, unloading the duffel bag onto the security post's desk. "Time tae get serious.

Chapter 24 — Lena Adderley — 23:05

She doesn't dare believe it.

After fighting her way from R&D to corporate, one look out of the first floor window confirmed her worst fears: they weren't going anywhere. Thousands of zombies are outside. They couldn't turn back, either, due to the multitudes of undead now loose in the compound, so up onto the roof was their only option. Soon enough, the zombies will break through the barricade she and Sofia erected. Yet now, a lifeline is in sight, in the form of a mystery party attacking the undead army from somewhere out front.

Of course, common sense dictates that one person can't destroy the whole horde. Lena and Sofia's reprieve will be short-lived, and they'll be torn limb from limb.

Unless it's Harry. If anyone could get the better of the monsters, it'd be him.

Adderley chastises herself. For a while, when she was younger, she wanted a lasting intimate relationship with Lunt to develop. She quickly learnt, however, that her father's head of security – a position Lunt lost when Grant Adderley learnt of the Scot's fling with Lena – was too one-dimensional. Too much of a follower who does as he's told, to the point where he would kill strangers if his employers deemed it necessary. Certainly, Lena can be cold-blooded, but only in defence of herself or family.

Also, if she does prevail, her survival will have been earned mainly by her own resourcefulness and determination, not Lunt's. She's been fighting for her life all day.

Bombs are exploding. Small ones, though, and they're not detonating amongst the dead.

"They're using grenades as a decoy." Sofia points. "Look, the zombies, they're being attracted away from the building."

"Like bait."

"Exactly."

"So we need to be ready to move. In case what he's doing works."

"You honestly think it's Lunt? He's not been answering his phone."

He won't abandon me. "I know. But whoever it is, they could be our ticket out of here."

"What about safe shutdown?"

"You said that was impossible."

Aslam's lips purse. "I've been thinking about it. I won't get too technical, but if I can get to the plant room, I think I might be able to fix it."

Lena watches as ninety percent of the horde below is provoked into a manic dash across the car park. "There's less than an hour left before this whole town is reduced to rubble. It'd be suicide."

"*I'll* be suicidal if I walk away from this without doing everything I can to prevent that missile strike. I was willing to lose my job to prevent this disaster, and now I'd be willing to lose my life to stop it getting worse."

Which is exactly the way I should feel. Except I don't. I want to survive, and I still cling onto the ridiculous hope that I can somehow save my family name from the dishonour which will destroy my dear old daddy. Does that make me a complete piece of shit?

She shivers. The sky has cleared; the temperature has dropped. The air is fresher out here, despite the faint whiff of dead flesh.

Now the zombies are at the gates. The gunfire and grenades have stopped, and some of the host are losing interest in their tormentor.

"Has he been caught?" Sofia wonders. "They're not firing anymore."

"I don't know. I can't —"

Suddenly, the guard post erupts in flame, as does a fuel tanker by the exit. Twin booms sound; by instinct, Lena and Sofia duck. The blast wave warms them, ruffles their hair, showers them with dust, but it does them no harm. Just sixty paces away, the swarm of ghouls between the security hut and the petroleum truck is not so lucky. Consumed by fire, at least half writhe as their flesh and clothes blacken.

"So that's what they were being lured into," Lena says, mesmerised by the blaze. After a moment, she remembers she's watching real people dance to their deaths, and she turns away. "Sofia! Where are you going?"

The running scientist is already halfway to the roof door. She waves but doesn't reply.

"Shit." *Should I go and help her? Or stick to Plan B?* The company director's not been idle-minded since they reached the roof. While Aslam's been occupied by altruistic dreams, trying to think of a way of safely neutralising Resurrex,

Lena's been racking her brains, desperate to devise a means of protecting her family name. By chance, she looked at the fence over which she climbed into the compound earlier. Seeing the compromised electric deterrent wire reminded her of the reason for its installation: eco-terrorists.

Said environmental zealots would make a plausible scapegoat for today's catastrophe. In recent times, climate change extremists have resorted to acts of sabotage against large corporations like Evolve. Although their cause is just, their proclivity for violence has been criticised by many. The general public, and more importantly the Government, will be content to blame such anarchists. Aslam would deny the claim, of course, but she'll be dead soon. Lena herself will know it's a lie, but her conscience will bear its telling. What good can come of the world learning the truth? What comfort will that bring anyone?

Movement in her peripheral vision brings her back to the present, and her stomach flips as she considers the fact that Sofia has cleared the blockage at the roof door. But when Lena sees the big man below her, equipped for war, she forgets the danger. For she is saved. "Harry!"

White teeth show in a face blackened by soot as he looks up. He's found a line of rope somewhere, and he's winding it into a tight coil. "Catch!" He launches the bundle towards her, just about getting it over the lip at the edge of the roof. "Where's Aslam?"

Lena shakes her head. "Gone." She stoops, grabs the rope and ties one end to a post bearing Evolve's tree-emblazoned flag. Then she straps the rifle to her back, though she's unsure whether there's any ammunition remaining in its magazine. Climbing down is harder than it appears. Her arms and shoulders ache, and her hands are raw by the time she reaches solid concrete. The man mountain waiting has to fire three times while she descends. Presumably, some of the creatures that survived the explosion are no longer distracted.

Harry takes Lena's rope-burnt hand and leads her towards the perimeter fence, using a pistol to slay any enemies that try to cut them off. Before long, they're outside the factory grounds. They make it to a black van parked nearby, where Lunt drags a black uniformed corpse from the driver seat, before either of the escapees speaks.

"You came," Lena pants, closing the passenger door.

"Aye." He starts the engine, then points a shotgun out of the window to blow away a zombie in pursuit. "Just doin' m' job." He releases the handbrake and puts his foot down. "What happened tae Aslam?"

She fastens her seatbelt. "She refused to come."

A muscle flexes in his jaw. "She's alive?"

"Yes."

"Why did she refuse tae come?"

Lena could lie, but after risking his life, Harry deserves the truth. So she tells him.

"Back there, when ye said 'gone', I thought ye meant dead. 'N' ah didn't know there might be a way o' shuttin' down. We could prevent even more damage bein' done!"

"There's no time. Those missiles will hit in thirty-five minutes. If she's not already dead, Aslam has no chance of doing whatever she plans to do in time. We just need… wait a minute, Harry, where are you going? It's left, not right… you're heading back *there*? To Evolve? This is insanity! She has no chance —"

"We can't just let her die, Lena. She's doin' the right thing, fer fucksake. So am I."

Lena can now see the car park fire again. *He's crazy. We were almost at the church, and now we're going back in there, with those* things!

"Ye don't have tae come wi' me. I'll drop ye off somewhere safe first. Villeneuve could just be bluffin', ye know. But whether he is or no', I cannae let a brave woman tryin' tae do the right thing die on her own."

"I thought you came for *me*!" She hates the self-pitying edge that creeps into her voice.

"Aye, ah did." Lunt runs over a zombie, then swerves a larger group. "But *you're* lookin' out fer yerself, while *she's* tryin' tae save lives. I couldnae live wi' m'self if ah left her tae save you."

"This is the wrong time to develop a moral conscience."

"Aye, well." Lunt brakes fifty yards short of Evolve plc's front gate. "Maybe these days I'm not as callous as ye said all those years ago. Anyway, am ah droppin' ye off nearby, or no'?"

Her mind has been whirring, her thoughts as murky as the reams of smoke billowing from the tanker fire up ahead. But now she finds absolute clarity. "No. You're right, Sofia should be rescued, and Villeneuve could be bluffing. I'll stay in the van, and cover you, or whatever."

"Ye sure?"

"Yes."

He grins and applies the accelerator. "Ye any good wi' that?" He nods at the carbine in her lap.

"I'm a quick learner."

Armed to the teeth, he decamps amidst the wreckage, dust and fumes. Immediately, he's shotgunning zombies, lobbing grenades and dashing towards the office's glass doors.

She clambers over the gear stick into the driver seat, a tear rolling down her cheek. As soon Lunt blasts his way into Corporate's lobby, Lena pushes down on the hand brake. "I'm sorry, Harry," she says, driving away from the man who came back for her.

But if she dies tonight, there will be no one to spread the cover story about eco-saboteurs causing the leak. *I owe it to my dad to do whatever I can to save the Adderley name. Family comes first.*

Chapter 25 — Luke Norman — 23:30

"He's there!" Jada points at the library's entrance.

Geraint's trying to break in to the building, but the doors won't budge. He turns to his pursuers with a pleading look on his face.

Luke's arms feel charged with energy, as if he's just been lifting weights. He crosses Chaucer Avenue, ignoring Gould's bus as it comes to a halt by The Ox and Cart. "Geraint," he calls, his step quickening. His own voice sounds disembodied. "Why ya runnin', Geraint?"

The ginger man shakes his head, then tries to break clear.

Brad, advancing from another angle, body tackles the older man and hits him in the gut.

Doubling over, Geraint salivates onto a cracked concrete flag. There's a tang of urine about him, and something else, something more seedy.

Luke seizes the man's bushy hair and straightens him up. Briefly, he pities Geraint. *He's terrified, like we're a buncha zombies.* Then he thinks of Connor, and righteous rage returns. "You know where he is, don't you?"

"Who? Who do you mean?" Geraint whimpers.

"Don't gimme that. My son, Connor."

"Why would *I* know?"

"You went really weird when you saw who we were on the bus. Why?"

"I… I was just shocked, I suppose. I thought everyone was dead. Then you came. I always thought everyone at work hated me, so when I got on, I thought you'd tell me to fuck off. And I'd be on my own again."

Shit. Have we got the wrong guy?

"That doesn't explain why you ran, Geraint," Jada says.

"Yeah," Brad chips in. "We didn't tell ya t' fuck off, did we? So why run?"

"I don't know! Maybe… I push people away 'cause I'm afraid of rejection. That's what my therapist says. And now that I'm ultra-stressed, I'm acting even weirder. That's all I can think of. But I know nothing about your son, and I hope he's okay."

Suddenly, Luke loses steam. He feels like sinking to his knees and surrendering, though he knows he should head back to Connor's mum's house to investigate the surrounding area. The chances of the kid being found are remote, but he can't give up. "What do ya think, guys? Is he tellin' the truth?"

Jada and Brad are non-committal.

"Honestly, I've done nothing wrong." Nursing his stomach, Geraint gets to his feet. "But I understand why you suspected me. I was acting weird, and I know everyone's more stressed than usual."

"Hang on a minute." Gould has got out of the bus. He's approaching with his revolver aimed at Geraint, who raises both hands. "He's lying."

"What? No, I'm not! I swear it!"

"Bollocks." Gould doesn't stop until the muzzle of his gun is inches from Geraint's fiery fringe. He cocks the hammer, then lowers his arm. "Tell the truth, pervert, or I'll shoot you in the balls and let you bleed to death."

The man at gunpoint begins to jabber, and the reek of piss strengthens.

"Woah, slow down," Luke protests, putting a hand on Gould's shoulder. "What makes ya so sure?"

"My friend assures me that this animal," he jabs the revolver barrel into Geraint's groin, "is lying. He knows where Luke's kid is, and if he doesn't tell us, I'll blow his penis off and feed it to him right now!"

"Calm down, bro!" Brad touches Gould's forearm, only for his hand to be shrugged away.

The security officer seems oblivious to everyone apart from the redheaded, cowering fellow before him. "I'm gonna count to three."

What should I do? Step in, or 'ope against 'ope that Gould does somehow know somethin', 'n' he'll lead us t' Connor?

"One!"

"Please!" Geraint looks at the others. "Stop him, you've got to stop him!"

"Josh, hear me out," Jada begins, in a detached, almost ethereal tone, "I know the voices in your head are tellin' you you're doin' the right thing. But you're not, okay?"

"Two!"

"Please, please, please!"

Jada raises her voice. "You need to ignore them, and listen to me."

Gould grits his teeth and spits, "Three!"

"Alright, okay!" Geraint babbles. "I know where Connor is, and I'll take you to him, right now! Just keep that psycho away from me!"

While Gould keeps his handgun trained on Geraint, Luke drives the bus. He grips the wheel till his knuckles are as white as the moon above Mortborough. *If that fuckin' paedo 'as 'urt Connor, I'll fuckin' feed 'im to the zombies myself.*

He pays no heed to the undead they pass on the way. The freaks are a sideshow now; his focus is on the evil perpetrated by the living. Geraint insists he's not harmed Connor, but he could be lying. Even if not, the boy is locked in a house, unable to run if the dead come calling.

Luke can't help thinking of the last time he saw his son. He argued with the boy's mother, caused a scene on her front lawn, embarrassed all three of them in front of the neighbours, almost started a fight with the new boyfriend Trent. And he can't even remember why. None of it matters now, though. There's a strong possibility that death has taken three of those four people on the lawn three weeks ago. Plus most, if not all, of the eavesdropping onlookers twitching at their curtains will be dead or undead.

The bed and breakfast is in even worse repair than it was when Luke stayed there, years ago. He didn't know Geraint's mother owned the place, nor did his co-worker ever mention his family business. *God knows what shenanigans they've been up to. Or did that sick fuck only start preyin' on kids when zombies caused anarchy?*

"I was just trying to protect them," Geraint says for the third or fourth time as Luke, Brad and Jada disembark.

Gould, who seems to relish the role of gaoler and is keeping watch on their sweating prisoner, has returned the guns taken from Lunt and Anderson.

A smattering of zombies are lurking in the street outside the hotel. As Luke helps his friends put the creatures out of their misery, he wonders if their presence is a promising sign or not. He fires the shots without thinking, hardly feeling the Sig Sauer recoiling in his hands. The gunfire is muted, the graphic scenes without colour in his eye, like reconstructions on TV rather than deeds of his own.

The daze intensifies as they storm the building. Catching sight of a large bloodstain on the kitchen floor hones his faculties for a moment, but by the time he's on the stairs, the trance has re-imposed itself. Jada and Brad are shouting Connor's name. So is Luke, he realises, though his voice sounds like it's not his own.

Then they're on the landing. Battering at a door. Children are shouting. The door busts open. A brown-skinned child appears, frothing at the mouth, wild-eyed, hissing like a riled cat. Jada's MP5 yammers. Blood squirts. Another door yawns. And there he is.

Connor, looking three years older, plus a girl; they're holding hands. Now Luke is embracing his boy, lifting him high, heedless of the indignation he's causing.

For a few short seconds, even with the zombie child bleeding at their feet, the apocalypse is forgotten.

Luke's elation is punctured by a shout from downstairs. Gould is at the door, gun in hand, with a stranger. "We need to leave."

"What's wrong?" says Jada as they descend to the ground floor.

"Guys, meet Ashara. She was riding past on a push bike. Ashara, meet the guys. They were in here, rescuing kids and killing zombies. Come on, get in the bus. We'll explain when we're moving."

A moment later, the bus is pulling away. Luke is sitting next to Connor, who appears agitated. "You okay, kid?"

"Where's Gary?" Connor's eyes are wide.

"You mean Geraint? Fair point." The PCV's interior still smells of the abductor's bowels. "Josh, where's that sick bastard Geraint?"

"I shot him." Gould doesn't take his eyes off the road. "He tried to escape when I was talking to Ashara."

Jada frowns.

"He's right," the Afro-Caribbean girl confirms. "The ginger dude tried to run."

"That's not important, anyway." The driver swerves to avoid something. "What's important is the missile strike coming our way. Midnight, right?"

Ashara nods. "That's what the big Scotch soldier said."

"'Scotch soldier'?" Brad, who's been staring forlornly at Luke and Connor, cocks his head to one side. "That'll be Lunt. He said nothin' 'bout no missiles."

"Well." Jada sitting beside Connor's female friend, speaks over the girl's head. "Better safe than sorry. If nothing happens at midnight, then we've lost nothing. If it does, we need to be as far away as possible. What time is it now?"

Connor looks at the smartwatch his dad gifted him. "Eleven fifty-nine. What about m' mum, though? The missiles'll kill her 'n' Trent."

Luke hugs his son close. "I'm sorry, Con, but yer mum's prob'ly... she might be..."

"Dead? I know. I just, like, forget sometimes. Or pretend. They're *all* dead, aren't they? Everyone in Mortborough apart from us."

"Maybe." Luke offers his most reassuring smile, but privately he's struggling to accept the likelihood that his hometown has died. "*We're* alive, though, Con. *We* made it out."

The eleven year-old says nothing. He reaches out to his left and takes Evie's hand.

The outskirts of the town are a blur of stalled cars, corpses and the walking dead.

"Look!" Brad gesticulates.

To their rear, in the distance yet rapidly getting closer, flying objects are bright in the night sky.

"The missiles," Jada says.

Up front, Gould accelerates. Three times they clip parked cars, and twice they plough through zombies too slow to react.

They're on the motorway slip road when the ordnance strikes. All of the passengers watch as their town is consumed by fire. A couple of sickening seconds later, a baritone rumble begins.

"It's over," Brad states. "It's all over."

Is it, though? Luke continues to stare at the ever-expanding fireball, hoping they've driven far enough to escape the bombardment.

Is it really over?

Printed in Poland
by Amazon Fulfillment
Poland Sp. z o.o., Wrocław

49379635R00125